BOOMTOWN

BOOMTOWN

Larry D. Names

THORNDIKE PRESS • THORNDIKE, MAINE

Library of Congress Cataloging in Publication Data:

Names, Larry D.
  Boomtown.

  1. Large type books. I. Title.
[PS3564.A545B59   1983)   813'.54   82-19694
ISBN 0-89621-429-X

Large Print edition available through arrangement with
Doubleday & Company, Inc.

Cover design by Armen Kojoyian.

DEDICATION

*To Paul and Arlene Krajac,
two beautiful people
who truly know the meaning
of friendship.*

BOOMTOWN

CHAPTER 1

Gold! Bright and shiny, it glistened between the grains of sand and the tiny pebbles in the washing pan. It was beautiful, delicious, delirious gold!

The crust of dirt on his skin and hair of his face cracked and flaked away as the prospector began to show the sudden excitement of the instant. The discovery of the yellow metal was a dream which most men shared but few saw come to reality. He was seeing it but not believing it completely until the rising exultation escaped his lips.

"Praise the Lord!" he screamed above the desert wind. "It's gold! I've found gold!"

Leaping to his feet, the man, barely past thirty but appearing to be well into middle age because of the countless days spent in the arid desert sun in search of the precious metal, went into a jubilant dance that had no rhythm

9

and no choreographed set of steps to follow. Leather boots that had been patched a dozen times clicked their heels in a frenzied jump. A tattered sombrero sailed wildly into the sky. Calloused hands reached for heaven in an effort to give thanks to the Almighty for delivering them from further drudgery. Knees that were sometimes sore and arthritic from too much kneeling along a hundred nameless streams were suddenly free of pain as they took every jolt of the bounding body.

But this wasn't the mother lode he had discovered. Russ Nichols knew about gold. The few grains he had found in the creek bed had been washed down from the mountains over countless centuries. Somewhere up above there was a vein that had given birth to these few particles. He would have to find that womb if he wanted to be rich.

It took the prospector a week to locate the hillside that held hidden wealth. He dug into earth for a few days to make certain that there was plenty of gold in the spot. After gathering samples, it took him another week to get to a town with an assayer in residence.

Lordsburg was little more than a way station for the Butterfield Stagecoach Line, but it did boast two saloons, a hotel with a restaurant, and a bank. Few people stopped there for more than an hour, and fewer spent the night. Mordecai Courtney was one of the latter.

Short in stature and very much on the lean side because of an asthmatic condition since childhood, Mordecai had come west for a number of reasons. The obvious was his health. The second was his occupation: journalist. At least he preferred to be called that. The other reasons were known only to Mordecai, and he wasn't telling anyone about them. It was rumored that an Indiana politician about whom Mordecai had seen fit to speak the truth, and in print no less, had given the newspaperman a set of choices: either leave the state permanently or leave the world for the same duration. Mordecai went west.

With a mule to carry his portable press and printing supplies tethered behind, Mordecai had set out on horseback across the wide expanse of the Plains in search of a town in need of a newspaper. Even a town that already had one would be suitable, providing of course that the forerunner could stand the competition. Thus far, he had been without good luck.

Lordsburg had a tabloid. Not a very good one by Mordecai's standards, but it was regular, which suited the few folks in the vicinity. Slightly disheartened, Mordecai decided to move on from New Mexico. Maybe there was something in Arizona for him.

Mordecai rocked in the saddle, lazily riding west out of Lordsburg just as Russ Nichols was strutting long strides ahead of his burro as he hastened eastward into the town. The two men noted the other's passing with casual, polite nods. Neither thought much of the other at first, but then Mordecai's instincts were stimulated. He looked back over his shoulder at Nichols, wondering why the man was in such a hurry. He reined up his horse and watched the prospector move down the street. Nichols made straight for the assayer's office.

A miner, thought Mordecai. A miner? Going into an assayer's office? Maybe he had found a new strike somewhere. Of course he had!

It was a story, and Mordecai Courtney never knowingly let a story pass him by.

He nudged his mount, simultaneously turning it back toward town. He followed Nichols' lead to the geologist's quarters. The prospector was already inside when Mordecai tied the horse to the rail out front. The journalist noted the gilt-edged gold lettering on the door glass, which read, Jordan Waters, Geologist and Assayer.

". . . looks good," the assayer was saying when Courtney stepped into the office unnoticed. "I'll have to assay it first to see how good."

12

"Go right ahead," said Nichols. "I'll wait right here."

"I'll wait, too," said Mordecai. Nichols turned around, and both men stared curiously at the short man by the door. "If you don't mind, that is."

"Who are you?" asked Nichols.

Mordecai smiled. "Courtney is the name, sir. Mordecai Courtney." He held out a hand to Nichols.

Russ Nichols was a tall man with a large frame. Next to Mordecai, he was a giant, a good foot higher above the ground. He accepted the greeting but with some reluctance.

"Nichols is mine. Russ Nichols."

"I'm glad to make your acquaintance, Mr. Nichols," said Mordecai as he pumped the stronger hand with both of his. He released the grip after the prospector gave a congenial nod. Mordecai cleared his throat before continuing. "After seeing you on the road, I watched you come into this office, and since I'm a journalist, my curiosity was aroused. Thus, my reason for being here. I'm wondering if you've made a new strike somewhere."

"Maybe I have," said Nichols warily, "and maybe I haven't."

"Well, I'd like to be the first to know if you have," said Mordecai.

"Sorry," said Waters. "You'll have to be second. I'm going to be first." He turned to the task at hand while the other two men continued the conversation.

"Yes, of course," stumbled Mordecai. "I meant the first after you two gentlemen."

"Why?" asked Nichols suspiciously.

"Like I said before, I'm a journalist."

"So what?"

"Well, I'd like to spread the news about your strike, uh, if there is a strike."

"Why?" asked Nichols again.

"It's my profession, Mr. Nichols."

"You got a newspaper here in Lordsburg?" asked the prospector.

"Bert Wooley owns the paper here in town," said Waters without looking up from his work.

"So I've been told," said Mordecai, "but if your strike is going to turn Lordsburg into a boomtown, then there might be room for two newspapers."

"You've got quite a find here," said the assayer unexpectedly. "Where did you locate these samples?"

"A week's walk north of here in the mountains," said Nichols. "Way up high. A little stream that trickles down to the Gila begins up there."

Mordecai produced a note pad and pencil

14

from inside his frock coat. He scribbled the prospector's latest words on the first blank sheet in the book.

"Well, you'd better get your claim registered right away," said Waters. "As soon as word gets out, you're going to have people all over those mountains."

"I'm fixing to head over there to the land office as soon as you tell me how good my ore is."

The assayer held up one chunk of rock. "This one runs about $1,500 to the ton." He put it down and hefted another. "This one maybe $4,000 a ton. The others about the same."

Nichols gathered up his samples and put them back into a pair of saddlebags. A smile finally broke out on his face.

"Looks like I'm going to be a rich man," he said. "Thank you, sir. I'd appreciate you not telling this around until after I've registered my claim." He dropped a $20 gold piece in the assayer's hand.

"I'll let Mr. Courtney here spread the word."

"Yes, thank you," said Mordecai as he looked up from his notes. "I'll be very happy to spread the word. With my first edition, of course. By the way, what are you going to call this mine of yours, Mr. Nichols?"

"The Lucky Nickel."

"I see. You're going to name it after yourself."

"Not quite. I'm going to spell it like the coin, not like my name."

"Very clever of you, Mr. Nichols. Very clever indeed."

Russ Nichols left the office, while Mordecai continued scratching notations on the pad.

"Looks like I'm going to be getting a lot of business now," said Waters.

"Why is that?" asked Mordecai.

"As soon as word gets out about this strike, the hills will be filled with men looking for gold. Most of them won't find any, but there will always be work in the mines where it is found. Nichols' discovery means there will be a whole new town up there in those mountains before too long, and that means I'll be moving up there where I can be close to the diggings. No matter how rich or poor the samples, the prospectors will have to bring them to me to be assayed."

"A new town, you say, Mr. Waters?" queried Mordecai.

"Always happens that way. Someone finds gold, a mining company moves in, and a whole town goes up. Almost overnight. It's the strangest thing you'll ever see."

16

"That's exactly what I plan to do," said Mordecai as he rushed for the door. "Thank you again, sir." He dashed through the portal to the outside in pursuit of Nichols.

"Mr. Nichols! Mr. Nichols!" he shouted after the prospector. He ran to catch Nichols, who was already twenty yards away down the street. Nichols turned around and waited for the journalist to come to him. Once he did, Mordecai strained to fill his lungs with life-giving breath before continuing. "Mr. Nichols, I have one more question for you. What are you going to call this place?"

"I've already told you that."

"No, I mean, what are you going to call the town that will grow up around your mine?"

"Hm. I haven't given it much thought." He stroked the stubble on his chin and stared at the vacant sky. "I don't rightly know what to call it." His eyes zeroed in on Mordecai. "Why don't you name it something? Yes, that's it. You name it, Mr. Courtney."

Nichols turned away and proceeded down the street, leaving Mordecai speechless for the moment. A blink of an eye later Mordecai collected his wits and again chased after the prospector.

"Wait, Mr. Nichols," squirmed the journalist at the prospector's heels. "I can't name a town."

17

"Sure you can," said Nichols as he kept walking, his long strides forcing Mordecai to trot in order to keep up with him. "It's easy. You just think up a name and give it to this place. See? Nothing to it."

"But it's your town or it will be once it's built. You should be the one to name it. That honor should belong only to you."

Nichols stopped as if frozen instantly. "What day is it?"

"Friday."

"Then I'll name the town Friday." Nichols resumed his pace.

"You can't name a town Friday," said Mordecai from behind him.

"That's what I'm going to name it if you won't do it."

Courtney caught up with Nichols again. "All right, you win. I'll name your town. We'll call it Nichols City."

"That's flattering, Mr. Courtney, but it won't do. I don't want it named after me."

"Then how about Courtney City?" Mordecai smiled.

"I don't want my town named after a runt like you," said Nichols. "No offense meant, of course, Mr. Courtney."

"Don't let it bother you. I've been called that since I was big enough to walk. I believe that was when I was three or four. I was a sickly child."

"You don't say."

"Yes, my childhood wasn't an easy one."

"You'll have to tell me about it someday," said Nichols as he brushed aside any further discussion of Mordecai's past.

"Yes, of course, we were talking about naming your town. Well, since you aren't fond of my name, how about calling it Lincoln after our late President?"

"New Mexico already has a town with that name."

"It does?"

"Besides, I'm from the South. I don't want my town named after any Yankee."

"Then how about Leesville?"

"He lost the war," said Nichols without missing a step.

Mordecai noticed that they were near the land office. He dashed in front of Nichols to slow him.

"Please, Mr. Nichols, this is a very serious matter."

"Why is it so serious, Mr. Courtney?"

"I have to know so I can put it on the head of my newspaper."

"But you don't have a newspaper."

"Ah, you are wrong, sir." Mordecai pointed

to his pack mule in front of the assayer's office. "There, sir, is my newspaper."

"Where?"

"All the equipment and supplies I need to put out a sheet are on that animal yonder. I can be set up in a few hours and have the first edition out a short time after that."

Nichols didn't believe him. He stared at Mordecai, then at the four-legged carrier in the distance.

"It's true, Mr. Nichols," said Mordecai, reading the prospector's thoughts. "A newspaper isn't a difficult proposition, but first it must have a name, a name which is usually derived from the town where it is published."

"I see," said Nichols. "Did you have a newspaper where you came from?"

"Yes, I did."

"And what was the name of that one?"

"The Frankfort *Gazette*."

"I don't like it." Nichols frowned.

"I'll admit that Frankfort isn't much of a name, but . . ."

"No, I mean, I don't like *Gazette*."

"I see," said Mordecai. "What newspaper name do you like?"

"I once saw one that had angels blowing trumpets on the top of it. I liked that one."

"*Clarion?*" offered Mordecai.

"That's it. *Clarion*. I thought that was a nice way to decorate the front page of a newspaper."

"I take it you can't read."

"Of course, I can read," snapped Nichols. "I went to school when I was young, the same as you did."

"No offense meant, Mr. Nichols," apologized Mordecai.

"None taken," said Nichols.

"Well, since you have an affection for *Clarion*, we'll have to come up with a name that goes with it. How about Gold Canyon?"

"No, every mining town gets named silver or gold something or other."

"Well, frankly, Mr. Nichols, I'm at a loss for words. I can't think of anything that might please you."

"Hold on a minute," interjected the prospector. "I once heard of a lost city that was supposed to be somewhere in these parts, but for the life of me, I can't recall the name of the place."

"A lost city?" mumbled Mordecai. "I don't know the name of any lost city."

"The place was supposed to have been burned to the ground, and then the folks who did the deed spread salt all over the ashes so nothing would ever grow there again."

Mordecai rolled his eyes. "I thought you said

21

you went to school."

"I did."

"Then you should know that it was the Romans who burned Carthage and . . ."

"That's it, Mr. Courtney!"

"Carthage?"

"Yes, Carthage. We'll call my town Carthage City, and you can call your newspaper the Carthage City *Clarion*."

Nichols slapped Mordecai on the shoulder and jostled him heavily. The journalist did his best to maintain his feet under the pressure.

"I suppose it'll have to do," said Mordecai. "Imagine it all, if you please. I had to come all the way from Indiana to build a newspaper named the *Clarion* in a town to be named Carthage City. I could have gone to Illinois and done that much."

"It'll be a good thing, Mr. Courtney," said Nichols. "Mark my words. It will be a good thing."

"Only if my newspaper says it'll be a good thing," said Mordecai, although slightly irritated. "Then and only then, Mr. Nichols."

CHAPTER 2

The first edition of the Carthage City *Clarion* was completely sold out before Mordecai Courtney departed Lordsburg. True to his word, the journalist had the sheet off the hand press within twenty-four hours after telling Russ Nichols he could do it, and an hour later all one hundred copies were in the hands of eager readers, everyone wanting to know about the new strike in the mountains north of the town.

Mordecai had set up his workroom in the back of the assayer's office, for a small price of course, and had worked throughout the night to get the job done. Like all good newspapermen, he had been prepared for such an occasion. Old stories, short items he had picked up during his travels west, advertisements he had gleaned from traveling salesmen, and a few fillers were already set in type when he arrived in Lordsburg. All he had to do to complete the first edition was to set the lettering in the head and write and set the lead story about Russ Nichols striking it rich. As soon as that was done, he was ready to print.

Before the ink was barely dry on the last single-page copy, Mordecai had repacked his mule and was ready to leave for the site of what would become Carthage City, New Mexico.

After registering his mining claim and an additional homestead claim to 160 acres of land in the Burro Mountains, Russ Nichols bought needed supplies at the general store and started back to his diggings that very same day. He knew what a gold rush was like. As soon as word spread, men from all walks of life would desert their daily routines, gather a few meager possessions, buy a few supplies, load it all on their own backs or that of an animal, and head in the general direction of the discovery. Gradually, they would all come together at the approximate location, and a mining camp would be born in the wilderness. Assayer Jordan Waters and journalist Mordecai Courtney had given Nichols a one-day head start on all those would-be claim jumpers.

Unlike all the others who were ready to pull up stakes and move to the new location in the mountains, Mordecai knew where he was going. He had convinced Russ Nichols to draw him a map of the route he would be taking. Because he was traveling on horseback and Nichols was afoot, leading his loaded-down burro, Mordecai was able to overtake the prospector on the second day out from Lordsburg.

"Hot today, Mr. Courtney," said Nichols in the way of a greeting. He hadn't taken the trouble to even look at Mordecai when speaking.

"That it is, Mr. Nichols," agreed Mordecai.

The journalist climbed down from the saddle and walked alongside his newfound companion. They stepped off another mile before speaking again.

"Folks must be all stirred up by now," said Nichols.

"It was quite a sensation." Mordecai smiled. He was thinking more of how he had scooped the local tabloid than he was of how the people had reacted to the news.

"Gold fever will do that, you know. It gets people all excited. Some even get to frothing at the mouth over it. I know, I used to be like that. Up in Colorado it was. Someone made a strike, and when it was told around Denver, nearly everyone in town dropped whatever it was they were doing at the time and headed straight for the mountains. No one knew exactly where they were going, but they were sure going to get there first no matter what it took. That's what gold fever does to a man. I wasn't much more than a boy then. I was hauling firewood for a fellow whose name I can't recall at this time. It was hard work, especially in the fall when everyone was storing up for the coming winter. Denver can get mighty cold in the winter. Anyway, I tagged along with a few fellows I knew, and we struck out for the mountains with a few supplies and fewer brains about what it takes to get the yellow stuff out of the ground. We were sure we were going to make a rich strike. All the way up those mountainsides we talked about it. We were talking about what we were going to do with all that money once we had it. I was going to go back to Carolina and buy myself a plantation and raise cotton. The war and a lack of gold put an end to that dream. We wound up working for a mining outfit. That's not the way to get rich."

"But now you've found it," said Mordecai. "You must be ready to fulfill that dream now."

"No, that dream is past. Now I dream of owning a big cattle ranch out on the Plains somewhere. I did a little cowpunching after the war, and I kind of got to liking it. It's hard work, but it beats digging in the earth all the time. Now mining is really hard work. I don't ever want to do that again. Oh, I'll work my own claim until some big mining outfit comes along and buys me out, but then I'm going to take my money and get me that ranch I've been dreaming about."

"Sounds like an admirable goal in life," said Mordecai.

"What are your plans, Mr. Courtney?" asked Nichols, showing an interest in Mordecai for the first time.

"Well, for the immediate future, I'm going to operate the Carthage City *Clarion*. After that, who knows? There might not even be an 'after that.' I just might spend the rest of my days in Carthage City."

Nichols allowed himself a soft chuckle. "Carthage City. Hell, man, there might not even be enough gold up there for one mine let alone enough to be building a whole town around. I may have just found a pocket that will pay out a few feet down."

"This news is disconcerting, Mr. Nichols." Mordecai sounded worried. "Why didn't you tell me this before?"

"Then again, this may be the richest strike ever known," said Nichols, ignoring Mordecai's question. "This may be the beginning of a new Denver. Ever been to Denver, Mr. Courtney?"

"I haven't had the pleasure."

"I was there almost from the start. Nothing there at first. Just a couple of streams that came together to make a river. People started coming in by the hundreds. Every day more people came until there was a whole city there. Thousands of people and every one of them hoping and praying to make it rich one way or another. Not too many of them ever made it or even came close. Who knows? It might be the same way with Carthage City. You just don't know how it's all going to turn out."

"For the better, let's sincerely hope, Mr. Nichols." As an afterthought, Mordecai added, "Of course, we should do everything within our means to help make that future a brighter one. Give it a helping hand, so to speak."

Nichols made no reply, so Mordecai discontinued the conversation until the prospector was ready to talk again. He had to wait until sundown.

"We'll spend the night here," said Nichols as he stopped walking near a small juniper tree. "The going gets harder from here on." He pointed at a sea-green mountain in the distance. "That's where we're headed. The land rises gentle from here to there, and then we go straight up the canyon."

"How much longer?" asked Mordecai.

"Another day to get to the canyon, and then another day after that to get up to my diggings."

Mordecai plopped himself on the ground and began rubbing his aching thighs. "I certainly hope it's all worthwhile. I would sorely hate to think I'm putting myself through all this for nothing."

"No one asked you along, Mr. Courtney," said Nichols as he removed a few eating utensils and some food from the pack on his burro.

"It's my duty, Mr. Nichols."

"How's that, Mr. Courtney?"

"I'm a journalist, and it's my duty in life to record the events of the day as they happen."

"Why?"

"To inform the public of what is happening around them."

"Why?"

"So they can be better informed." Mordecai shrugged.

"What for?" Nichols began gathering twigs and grass to make a fire.

"So they can survive in this world." Mordecai struggled to his feet, although he wanted to jump up as he realized that he had the upper hand in the discussion. "How would a man know that you've struck gold in those mountains if my newspaper hadn't told him?"

"Someone I would've told would've blabbed it sooner or later. Tongues do wag, Mr. Courtney."

Mordecai joined Nichols in gathering the firewood.

"Yes, but how accurate are they? How many times does a story change when it is passed on from mouth to ear? It's possible that every teller of the same tale can change it with each telling. It can go on until the truth of the original story is lost in exaggeration. But, my new friend, in a newspaper the words are printed for the eyes to see and the brain to decipher until the true meaning is made to the reader. Those printed words never change. As long as the paper they're printed on lasts, those words will always remain the same."

"Or until someone goes to copying them," added Nichols.

"To copy means to make an exact replica," Mordecai retorted.

"You have me there, Mr. Courtney."

Nichols struck a match and touched the flame to a bunch of grass. As it flared, he added a few small twigs, then larger sticks until the fire was ready for the coffeepot. He opened two cans of beans and poured them into a blackened skillet for heating. He cut two slices of bacon from a side and added them to the beans.

By dark, the meal was ready to be consumed.

They ate without conversation, then wiped the tin plates clean. Water was too precious in that arid land to use for washing dishes. Mordecai rolled out two blankets; one to go between him and the ground and the other to cover him. Nichols crawled beneath an elk robe.

"Tell me, Mr. Nichols," said Mordecai, "don't you find it lonely and sometimes fearful being out here alone?"

"I don't have time to worry about such nonsense," growled Nichols. He was ready for sleep, and Mordecai's questions were keeping him from it.

"But what about Indians?"

"Do you see any Indians, Mr. Courtney?" asked Nichols, raising himself up on one elbow.

"No, but . . ."

"Nor do I, but I do see that it's dark. That means it's time to sleep. Do you get my meaning, Mr. Courtney?"

"Good night, Mr. Nichols."

Mordecai rode his horse most of the next day and all of the day after. Just as Nichols had said, the land rose slightly until they reached the canyon carved into the side of the mountain by the little stream that ran down to the

Gila River. The smallest hint of a trail followed the course of the trickling waterway, and although sometimes treacherous, it wasn't as hard to follow as Mordecai had imagined from Nichols' description of it.

"My diggings are just around the next bend," announced Nichols near day's end. "You won't know they're there until we come right up on them. I chopped down a pine tree that fell over them to keep anyone who might happen up this way from finding my claim."

"That was very clever," acknowledged Mordecai.

"Yes, it was," said Nichols. "I could've just cut off a few branches to cover the hole, but that was too easy. A good man who sees a pile of pine boughs is sure to look under them. But a cut-down tree? No one would ever think of looking under a fallen tree for a mine."

Mordecai clucked his tongue as he surveyed the immediate vicinity. He shook his head as if he was arguing with himself over a perplexing problem.

"Something wrong, Mr. Courtney?" asked Nichols, showing an increasing interest in his traveling companion.

"Well, it seems to me that the canyon is too steep for the building of a town," said Mordecai, still looking about.

"This canyon is, but the one around the bend just might be the right place to build a town. The slope is more gentle, and the stream runs right down the middle of it. There might not be much room for side streets, but there's plenty of space for a nice boulevard to run on each side of the stream."

"By the way," said Mordecai, "what is this stream called?"

"It doesn't have a name that I know of."

"Then we'll call it Courtney Creek."

"That seems fair enough. The size of the thing matches you." Nichols bent down next to the clear flow of water and scooped up a handful. He poured it back and said, "I christen thee Courtney Creek."

"Can you do that?" asked Mordecai.

"I found it, so I guess I can name it what I want."

The sun was a giant orange resting atop a distant peak. The two men turned around to watch the last rays of daylight fade from yellow to dark red.

"Look down there," said Nichols. "You see all those little white dots on the plain?"

"Yes?"

"Campfires. Must be a couple dozen of them. Those are the first men to follow us up here. Tomorrow about this time, the hills will be crawling with them. You'll have plenty of readers for your next edition of the Carthage City *Clarion*, Mr. Courtney."

"I didn't think they would come this soon."

"Sure they will. Day after tomorrow some enterprising fellow will be up here with a keg of beer and a case of whiskey. He'll water down the whiskey and sell it for ten times what he paid for it. He's one of the men who will make it rich."

"As will you and I," said Mordecai.

"How do you figure yourself in on this?" quizzed Nichols.

"We have a town to sell," said Mordecai with a sly grin that gave him an elfin appearance.

"No, we don't have a town to sell. I want no part of that. It was your notion to have a town up here, not mine. You sell it, Mr. Courtney."

"But it's your strike, Mr. Nichols."

"The mine belongs to me, but the town is yours. I give it to you here and now." Nichols pulled a piece of paper from inside his coat and thrust it at Mordecai. "You lay it out, and you sell it. I have no time for it."

Mordecai accepted the deed and glanced at it.

"But there is wealth to be made selling lots," he protested.

"I agree, Mr. Courtney, and you are wel-

34

come to it. As for me, I will get my gold from the ground. You can get yours from the greenhorns."

As such a bargain was struck between the two men, Mordecai Courtney became the midwife in the birth of Carthage City, New Mexico.

CHAPTER 3

A prophet, that's what Russ Nichols should have been. He had seen the immediate future and had declared it to Mordecai. The journalist had marked the prospector's words, then watched them all come true. Maybe not in specific terms, but overall, Nichols hadn't missed a card.

While there was still time before the first arrivals, Mordecai spent his first day in Carthage City marking off lots for various businesses that he was certain would come to the fledgling town. A courthouse would be the dominant feature of the new municipality. Across from it, a hotel with a fine restaurant. Large lots for both of these structures. Next to the government house would be his own establishment, the Courtney Building, which would be the home of the *Clarion*. Up the street, there was plenty of room for stores, saloons, and offices. Behind them and farther up the canyon, the residential section could be built. It was a grand plan he had, but only Mordecai Courtney had it.

As sundown approached, the third citizen of Carthage City made his way into the town limits delineated by the deed Nichols had given to Mordecai. Riding one horse and leading a second loaded down with a double pack, the stranger turned the bend and made straight for the campsite that Mordecai was sharing with Nichols. Bearded, heavyset, and of average height, the man wore a black frock coat, matching pants, knee boots, and a bowler.

A businessman, thought Mordecai on first inspection. He and the prospector were sitting cross-legged by the fire, drinking coffee, while their evening repast of beans and bacon bubbled and crackled above the flames.

"That would be our whiskey peddler," said Nichols after a brief once-over.

"How do you know for sure?" asked Mordecai.

"Ask him," said Nichols passively.

"All right, I will." Mordecai stood as tall he could in an effort to be impressive. His size limited the attempt. "Good evening, sir," he said as the newcomer halted his animals short of the journalist.

"The same to you, sir," replied the mounted man in a gravelly voice. "Would this be Carthage City?"

"This is where it'll be built," said Mordecai proudly.

"Humph!" grunted the horseman. "Sure is out of the way. You can't even see down in the valley from here."

"A mistake on the part of Mother Nature, sir," said Mordecai.

"Maybe a mistake on mine, too." He scanned the immediate area before resuming the conversation. "What are all them notches for?"

Mordecai had taken the liberty of chopping crosses into a number of tree trunks in order to designate various lots.

"Are you interested in purchasing a lot in our fair city, sir?" inquired the would-be land dealer.

"You holding the paper on this land?" asked the man, who still sat in the saddle.

"He isn't," said Nichols, entering the discourse, "but I am." The prospector casually shaved a sliver off a stick of wood with a bowie knife as he spoke. "Mr. Courtney here is acting as my agent. You can deal with him in the matter of land purchasing."

"I see," said the stranger, careful to note the rough exterior of Nichols as well as the large blade that had a reputation of being the only weapon a man needed in order to hunt bears. "Well, Mr. Courtney, I'm looking for a place to locate my saloon."

"I told you he was a whiskey peddler," said Nichols without looking up from his whittling.

"Well, yes, Mr. . . . ?" Mordecai hesitated.

"Bemis is the name, Mr. Courtney. George Bemis. I was working the bar in the California House in Lordsburg when I read your newspaper and saw the story about Mr. Nichols' strike up here."

"And you followed our trail just like all them other fellows who are right now climbing up the canyon," said Nichols. "Is that not so, Mr. Bemis?"

"A very astute observation, Mr. Nichols," said Bemis.

"There was nothing astute about it," retorted Nichols. He flicked a long splinter into the fire. "It always happens that way. One man finds gold, and everyone goes to frothing at the mouth in an effort to claim the land around his. There's nothing astute about that."

"Yes," interrupted Mordecai. He cleared his throat. "Now about that lot."

"Put him over there someplace," said Nichols, motioning with a jerk of his head toward the other side of the stream. "Put him

39

and all his kind on that side of the creek. It's always best to group these kind of people."

"That's not exactly a friendly attitude, Mr. Nichols," said Bemis.

The prospector looked up at the newcomer for the first time. "You've gotten my meaning then, Mr. Bemis. I don't drink myself, and if I could prevent it, I would stop all men from drinking. I know I can't, so I keep myself away from whiskey and people who sell the stuff. There will be plenty of men up here in the next few days to keep you busy enough, Mr. Bemis, but they will keep you busy on the other side of the street."

"You've made yourself perfectly clear, Mr. Nichols," said Bemis, "and I'll abide by your decree. One place is as good as another."

"Good. I'm glad that's clear. Sell him a lot, Mr. Courtney."

"What is your asking price, Mr. Courtney?" inquired Bemis.

"Not very much," said Mordecai. "A mere two hundred dollars."

"Too high."

Mordecai was taken aback. "Too high, you say?"

"I believe those were my very words, sir."

"I assure you, Mr. Bemis, that two hundred is a very fair price. Why in less than a week, the standard will be three or four times that. Surely, you can see that your money will be well invested."

"I still say too high," argued Bemis.

At that moment another man riding a horse and trailing two burros behind him rounded the bend into Carthage City. Nichols was the first to see the second stranger.

"The price goes up to three hundred in five minutes, Mr. Bemis," said Nichols as he casually pointed the bowie knife toward the approaching rider. "I'll wager that man will gladly pay it just to have the first saloon in Carthage City."

Bemis turned in the saddle to view the new man. He twisted back to Mordecai in an instant.

"Two hundred it is then," said Bemis. He reached into his coat for some money. He held out a $20 bill to Mordecai, who reached for it. "Twenty now and the rest as soon as I sell my wares."

"That's a bad bargain, Mr. Bemis," interrupted Nichols. "You haven't established any credit in this town yet."

"But this is all I have," demurred Bemis.

"Maybe that other man has more, Mr. Courtney," said Nichols. "You might want to wait a few minutes before closing this game."

"An excellent idea, Mr. Nichols," said Mordecai.

"No, wait." Bemis squirmed. "I might have more." He made a show of searching all his pockets. "Yes, I believe I have." Almost magically, he produced a wad of notes. "Here, payment in full."

Mordecai took the roll and counted it. Nine more twenties brought the total to two hundred dollars.

"The property is yours, Mr. Bemis," said Mordecai, satisfied that he had concluded a favorable transaction.

"Don't I get a deed or something in writing that says which lot I own?" requested Bemis.

"A deed? I hadn't thought of that," said the journalist-turned-real estate agent.

"Scratch out a bill of sale on some of that paper of yours, Mr. Courtney," said Nichols. "That should do until we establish a proper land office here."

Mordecai hurried to prepare the document, quickly determining that Bemis should have lot Number 1 in Block Number 6. That would put the saloon far enough away from the proposed courthouse and on the opposite side of the street. He presented the deed to Bemis just as the second stranger rode into the camp.

"I'll show you your lot first thing tomorrow

morning," said Mordecai as he handed the paper up to Bemis. Then he turned to greet the newcomer, who halted his mount close to Bemis. "Welcome to Carthage City, sir."

"Good evening, gents," said the new arrival. He removed his brown felt hat and wiped his forehead with the sleeve of a like-colored, cotton, short coat. His hairline was receded a few inches up his pate. A droopy black mustache blanketed his upper lip. He didn't look to be much past thirty years old, and as he sat in the saddle, it was difficult to denote that he was of average height.

"It's a long ride up here, isn't it?" considered the new man.

"And well worth it." Mordecai smiled.

"That is a matter for further conjecture," snorted Bemis. "I'll see you in the morning, Mr. Courtney." He rode off up the canyon.

"Not a very friendly sort, I gather," said the newcomer after Bemis was out of earshot.

"But he's a satisfied customer," replied Mordecai. "Now what can I do for you, sir?"

"He's looking for a place to build a store; dry goods more than likely," Nichols answered for the man.

"That's quite correct, sir. Harry Willit is my name, and I've come from Silver City to open a dry-goods store in this place."

Mordecai was dumbfounded. Nichols had given him the idea that this second man, Willit, was another saloonkeeper, and suddenly he discovered that he was misled.

"Mr. Nichols, I thought this man was . . ."

"So did Bemis," said Nichols with just a hint of a grin at one corner of his mouth.

It took Mordecai another second to comprehend the devious design that Nichols had woven over the negotiations with Bemis, and as soon as he had all the particulars straight in his head, Mordecai nearly laughed.

"Yes, indeed, Mr. Nichols. So he did." Mordecai had to shake off the mirth of the moment before continuing with Willit. "A dry-goods store, you say, Mr. Willit. Well, every town needs a dry-goods store, and I happen to have a very favorable lot available for just such an establishment."

"Then I take it you have already staked a claim on this land?" asked Willit.

"Mr. Nichols has, sir," said Mordecai, waving a hand in the prospector's direction. "One hundred and sixty acres. All that lies between the ridges on either side of this stream. I'm Mordecai Courtney. I own the Carthage City *Clarion*."

"A newspaper already," said Willit, a little impressed. "That's a very positive sign that this will be a permanent town. How much for the lot you mentioned?"

"Two hundred dollars."

"A reasonable price," said Willit.

"Climb down and join us," said Nichols. "You're welcome to share our meal."

"Thank you, sir," said Willit. "It's nice to find such hospitality in the wilderness." He dismounted and tied his horse to a nearby tree. "Now about this lot, which one would be mine?"

Mordecai started to motion across the creek, but he was cut short.

"Your horse is standing on it," said Nichols.

"Very good indeed, sir," said Willit.

Mordecai was confused. He wondered how Nichols knew which lot he had set aside for the first store. He hadn't said anything to him about which one was for what.

"A choice location, Mr. Courtney," said Willit. "I thank you."

The deal was closed in cash, and Mordecai wrote out another bill of sale for the purchase.

After the evening repast, Willit unloaded his pack animals, affording Mordecai and Nichols a few minutes for a private conversation.

"For someone who wanted nothing to do with selling lots and building a town," began Mordecai, "you've sure made me think the opposite."

"Well, don't," said Nichols as he crawled beneath his elk robe. "I was just giving you a helping hand with the first two. If I hadn't, Bemis over there would have got his land for nothing, and then you would've put Willit on the wrong side of the creek because you thought I wanted it that way. I heard you mumbling to yourself this afternoon about where you wanted the general store to be. That's an awful bad habit, Mordecai Courtney. You should best beware that the wrong people don't hear you rambling on like that. You could get yourself in a lot of trouble."

"You astound me, Mr. Nichols," said Mordecai as he shook his head.

"That's not too hard a thing to do, Mr. Courtney, considering who you are and who I am."

"Yes, I can see that, too," said Mordecai, not taking offense. "You might say that I'm one of those greenhorns you mentioned earlier."

"Most assuredly so, Mr. Courtney." Nichols rolled his back to Mordecai. "See you in the morning."

"Good night, Mr. Nichols."

Willit returned to his place beside the campfire.

"Chilly up here in the mountains," he observed as he sat down and crossed his legs.

The firelight made a ghostly dance on his pale skin. His mustache appeared to be a black gash beneath a bulbous nose. Even when he spoke it looked more like a hole in his face than a growth of hair. "I'll have to remember to get in a supply of heavy clothing."

"You said you were from Silver City, Mr. Willit," said Mordecai. "I'm a newcomer to these parts, and I'm not familiar with that town."

"Silver City lies to the northeast of here," explained Willit. "It's actually closer than Lordsburg. I received news of this place just three days ago, and I immediately set out for it. I own a store in Silver City. I left it in the care of my wife and children. They can run it until such time as I see fit to sell or until I return. I've even thought of keeping both places, if everything works out as I hope."

"Carthage City is on the verge of becoming a great city in these parts, Mr. Willit. Mr. Nichols' discovery is only the first in these mountains. I'm certain many prospectors will find a bonanza or two in this vicinity, and then the mining companies will come, bringing in more people. Before too long we'll have a thriving city."

"Let's hope those are prophetic words, Mr. Courtney, and not just the overzealous prattles of a newspaperman."

Mordecai was accustomed to such abuse. "Time will tell, Mr. Willit. Time will tell."

CHAPTER 4

The following week saw more than a hundred men move into Carthage City. However, only four more lots were sold by Mordecai, but several were leased with options to buy. As a town, the area paralleling Courtney Creek in the Burro Mountains was beginning to take shape.

The second edition of the *Clarion* was printed in a tent that Mordecai had purchased from Harry Willit. The storekeeper had sold out all the goods he had initially brought to Carthage City, and Mordecai reported the good news in the newspaper. Also, on the same front page was a story about the evils of alcohol. Mordecai Courtney was no mover for temperance, but seeing that Russ Nichols was and since he wanted to remain on the better side of the prospector, the journalist ran the article. In order to keep on the right side of

George Bemis, he had another item on the back page which extolled the fine quality of the saloon's wares.

Russ Nichols kept to himself most of the time, only visiting Mordecai in the evening, usually for supper. Nichols wasn't fond of cooking, whereas Mordecai enjoyed preparing his own meals, but more so, he delighted in sharing his culinary triumphs with a guest. Since Nichols was so willing to permit Mordecai to retain all the funds from the land sales and leases, the newspaperman felt that he should make such a minor reciprocation.

The night before departing for Silver City for another load of supplies and dry goods Harry Willit met with Nichols and Courtney in the latter's tent. He immediately came to the point of his visit, but after making the initial announcement of the trip and its purpose, he noted that Mordecai appeared to be quite dejected. He quickly added that he fully intended to return to Carthage City as soon as possible with a larger store of goods.

"I'm very much relieved to hear that," said Mordecai.

"Please forgive the dramatics, Mordecai," said Willit. "They were quite unintentional."

"Bringing back more goods, you say," said Nichols. "A wagonload, correct?"

"That was my plan, Mr. Nichols."

"But you can't get a wagon up here, Mr. Nichols," said Mordecai.

"I'm glad you noticed that, Mordecai," said Nichols. "Of course, he can't get a wagon up here. He needs a road for that."

"But we don't have a road," said Mordecai.

"Then we'll have to build one."

"Build one? How?"

"Tomorrow morning before everyone leaves for their diggings, you call a meeting of all the men and explain to them how we need a road up here."

The next morning the miners gathered in front of Mordecai's tent. There was no way to describe them collectively. Some were small, some large, most average height. Very few were overweight. Their clothing was about as similar. Mexican sombreros, bowlers, Stetsons, engineer's caps, military visors, stovepipes, stocking caps — they were all there. Open vests, leather and cloth short coats, several colors in frock coats, buckskins, woolen shirts — both dyed and white — adorned the gold seekers. Knee boots, half boots, high-top shoes, moccasins, cowboy boots — a complete variety of footwear. Not all were bearded or mustachioed. The only similarity they all knew was dirt. There wasn't a man among their count who didn't need a bath in the worst way, but since they were all in that condition, no one knew it but the wild animals.

Mordecai raised his hands to quiet the chattering crowd. When that didn't work, he called for their attention. Still no success. It had to be his size. Mordecai simply didn't command anyone's respect on sight.

Seeing the difficulty the journalist was having, Russ Nichols stepped to the front of the gathering. He was taller than almost every man there, but to emphasize his stature, Nichols stood on a flat boulder off to one side of Mordecai. He didn't raise his hands or verbally request silence. He simply scowled at the first man whose eye he caught. Nichols bored his stare into the man's brain, forcing the onlooker into an aphonia that was contagious. The victim of the prospector's glowering orbic intrusion nudged his neighbor with an elbow. The gent standing next to him peered at his friend first, then followed his eyes to Nichols. He also dropped his speech, and like a dying wave on a sandy beach, the miners were hushed.

"They're all yours, Mordecai," said Nichols as he gave his stone platform over to the newspaperman.

Mordecai, also in awe of the man, moved

with hesitation to replace Nichols at the head of the meeting. A slight jerk of Nichols' head beckoned the journalist to take charge. Courtney complied.

"Gentlemen, now that I have your attention," began Mordecai, "I'll get right to the purpose of this town meeting."

"I wish you would," interrupted one miner. "I've got work to get to."

Nichols twisted slowly until both his eyes cut into the man's skull. The look said no more such outbursts would be tolerated.

"We've all got work to do," said Mordecai, feeling the strength of having Nichols to back him. "Carthage City needs a road, gents. We need a road up here from the valley. The trail is fine for horses and pack animals, but we need a road for wagons to use. Mr. Willit, the storekeeper, plans to bring a wagonload of supplies back from Silver City, but he needs a road to get all his goods up here in one trip."

"Let him build his own road," shouted one man. That set off a general growl of agreement.

"Gentlemen, gentlemen," Mordecai pleaded for their attention. Without Nichols' assistance, the group quieted. "Gentlemen, the road is necessary for everyone to use. How do you plan to get your ore out of here? On the backs of your horses and mules? No, of course not. You'll need wagons to haul it out."

"The little fellow's right," said a man at the rear of the gathering. "We got to have a road. How do you propose we build this road, sir?"

"I'm glad you said 'we.' That's exactly what we have to do. We have to build this road. Every man here must do his share for the benefit of all."

"Such as?" asked the same man.

"We'll have to organize first," said Mordecai.

"Who's going to be in charge of this?" was asked.

"I propose Mr. Courtney be elected to the post," said George Bemis. "Sooner or later this town's going to need some sort of government, so why don't we elect Mr. Courtney as mayor until we can have a regular election? He seems to have all the right ideas."

There was a ripple of chatter spreading through the men.

"I second that motion," said Russ Nichols above the din. "Mordecai Courtney for mayor of Carthage City."

A few shouts of approval were heard, followed by some cheers and applause.

"Let's take a vote," was heard. "All in favor of the little fellow being the mayor of Carthage City signify by shouting aye."

A thunder of affirmatives followed.

"All opposed keep quiet."

Laughter rumbled forth.

"Done then. Mordecai Courtney is the first mayor of Carthage City."

Approving talk circulated through the crowd, which to Mordecai's dismay began to drift away.

"Gentlemen, we haven't settled the matter of the road," shouted Mordecai.

"It's your problem now, Mr. Mayor," said the same man back to him. "You solve it."

Mordecai appealed to the men to remain and continue the meeting, but few listened. George Bemis and Russ Nichols were two who stayed.

"You payed out on that one, Mordecai," deplored Nichols.

"All isn't lost, Mr. Courtney," said Bemis. "You are the mayor now."

"Yes, I'm the mayor," lamented Mordecai. He was dejected, a feeling that exhibited itself outwardly, making the journalist appear to be smaller than ever. He fell into a mild catatonia.

"Mr. Bemis, I've found a sudden new respect for you," said Nichols. "I can see that you've got a plan, and I think it matches mine."

"A tax, Mr. Nichols?" Bemis smiled.

"Precisely," said Nichols with a wink.

"Mr. Mayor, since you are the government

in Carthage City," began Bemis, "I would like to make a suggestion." He noted that Mordecai was inattentive. "Mr. Courtney?"

"Hm? Yes?"

"As I was saying . . ." said Bemis, but he didn't get to continue.

"Bemis here was saying you ought to tax the good citizens of Carthage City in order to build the road," said Nichols.

"Exactly," agreed Bemis. "Levy a tax to pay for the road."

"And those who can't pay in cash," continued Nichols, "they can pay in labor. That's how you'll get your road built, Mordecai."

A flame was rekindled in Mordecai's eyes. "Yes, I see. Since I'm the mayor, I can do most anything I want, can't I?"

"Within limitations, Mordecai," cautioned Nichols. "Those men who elected you? They can unelect you, too."

"Don't worry yourself over me, Mr. Nichols," said Mordecai. "I can take care of this. Excuse me, gentlemen. I have a newspaper to get out."

Mordecai disappeared into his tent. Bemis and Nichols turned away in separate directions.

The newspaperman spent the day setting type and printing the third edition of the

Carthage City *Clarion*. The number featured the mayoral election and the new official's proclamation of the highway tax.

The initial reaction to Mordecai's tax was anger. The citizenry of Carthage City was fired up and ready to depose the mayor of one day. Fortunately for Mordecai's political ambitions, cooler heads held the sway of the miners. As soon as one was asked who was going to enforce the new law, everyone realized that Mordecai was a lion with no teeth. Little did they know that Russ Nichols and George Bemis were fashioning a new set of chompers for the diminutive mayor.

"Mr. Nichols, I can see that this town is going to amount to something," said Bemis over the bar inside his tent saloon. "That is, it will as long as the gold holds out."

"There's plenty of gold in these mountains, Bemis," said Nichols. "There's no need to worry over it running out too soon."

"Thank you for your assurance of that fact. Now I can go ahead with the next step in my plans."

"Which is?"

"I'm going to construct a permanent building for my saloon."

"How big a place do you intend to build?"

"There'll be room for gambling tables and a full-length bar."

"I expected that much, Bemis, but will there be rooms in a second story?"

"Why, Mr. Nichols, are you suggesting that I hire ladies to entertain my customers in ways other than song and dance?"

"I don't hold with women selling themselves, Bemis," said Nichols, "but just like liquor, there's nothing I can do about it. I was just thinking that if you let it be known that you intend to bring ladies up here as soon as you get your saloon built, it might be helpful to our short friend."

"How do you mean?"

"Well, it would seem to me that in order to get everything you'd need to complete your establishment you'd first have to have a road on which wagons could travel in order to get it all up here. Don't you agree?"

Bemis smiled. "I understand you completely, sir."

"Good night, Mr. Bemis," said Nichols as he left the bar.

The next morning Mordecai was awakened by a dozen voices in half as many conversations which were going on outside his tent. After slipping on his pants, he stumbled groggily to the entrance and peeked through the tent flaps. A gang of miners was milling about nearby. He wondered if they meant him any harm.

"There he is," said a man who saw the journalist having a look-see at the mild commotion. "Come on out, Mayor."

Others voiced the same request, and Mordecai, brave beyond his size, pushed the canvas apart and boldly walked outside.

"Is something wrong?" he inquired sternly.

"We've come to pay our taxes," said the man closest to him.

"What?" blurted Mordecai.

"We've come to pay our taxes," the man repeated.

"That's what I thought you said." Mordecai was certain that he was still lying between his blankets fast asleep. This wasn't really happening, he told himself.

But it was. George Bemis had made it perfectly clear that he wasn't going to bring any ladies to Carthage City until his saloon was built and that couldn't happen unless wagons could haul up the needed materials. The miners understood the rest without being told.

Work was begun on the road that very day as each man who didn't have the ten dollars which had been levied for the purpose of the project took up an ax, shovel, or pick and labored on the thoroughfare. Mordecai, after appointing himself as superintendent of public works, supervised the miners-cum-road builders. In an effort to show that he was a capable leader, the journalist-mayor helped wherever he thought he was needed, which wasn't in too many places. By the end of the day the workmen had completed a little more than a hundred yards. They were off to a good start by Mordecai's standards.

That night a few of the miners who had worked on the roadway gathered at Bemis' saloon. It didn't take long for the discussion to turn toward the subject of politics.

"That little runt could turn into a dictator real quick," said Deke McCatty, a burly man of average height sporting a salt-and-pepper beard and wearing buckskin. "If we don't do something to stop him right now, he might make some law that could lead to real trouble."

"McCatty's right," piped up Frank White. He looked like a farmer and in fact had been one before the war. Although years later, and long after he had given up the plow and scythe, White held fast to his heritage of self-dependence. "I don't want anyone making any laws that I don't have a say in."

George Bemis leaned both of his hands on the plank that served as a bar as he listened to the conversation. Bemis was an honest man, but that wasn't to say he wouldn't take advantage of an opportunity if given the chance.

Money was his main concern in life.

"Gentlemen, if you're that worried about our esteemed mayor," offered Bemis, "then I should think that another meeting is in order."

"Yeah," said McCatty, "and we can vote the little runt out of office."

"No, gentlemen, that wouldn't be necessary," said Bemis. "Besides, he hasn't done anything that requires such action."

"I suppose you're right," said White. "What did you have in mind, Mr. Bemis?"

"Call the miners together, and I'll make my thoughts known to everyone at the same time."

Within minutes every man in the camp was assembled outside Mordecai's tent. Torches were lit to provide light, and the men peacefully awaited the mayor to begin the meeting.

"What is the purpose of this gathering?" asked Mordecai, unaware of the earlier conversation in the saloon.

"I called this meeting," said Bemis.

"It figures," mumbled Russ Nichols. He had been disturbed from his slumber and would have forgone the event if not for the fact that he knew Mordecai would be at the mercy of the miners without him. He sat on a stump a few feet away from the mayor.

"Since we have the beginnings of a real town here," began Bemis, "a few of us thought it would be best that we have a legal governing body. A town council, if you will."

Several men, although hearing of the proposal for the first time, voiced their approval immediately with shouts of agreement. Mordecai held up his hands to maintain order.

"Gentlemen, please let Mr. Bemis finish," ordered Courtney.

The crowd settled down again.

"I think we should have an election as soon as possible," said Bemis.

"I wholeheartedly concur, Mr. Bemis," said Mordecai. "We should be practicing democracy here in Carthage City and right from the start. First off, we have other business to tend to."

"Such as?" asked McCatty suspiciously.

"Well, first we have to decide how many men we want to sit on this council," said Mordecai.

"That makes sense," said White. "What do you say, Mr. Bemis?"

"Nine," said Russ Nichols, not giving Bemis a chance to answer.

Bemis studied the prospector before speaking. "Yes, nine should be the number of men to handle the affairs of our town. I propose that the town council of Carthage City consist of nine members, each to be elected by the entire population of Carthage City and its immediate vicinity."

"Let's vote on it," said McCatty.

"You've all heard the motion by Mr. Bemis," said Mordecai. He called for the vote, and the proposition was carried unanimously. "Now to the business of an election. I think we should hold it right here and now."

The miners were surprised by the mayor's statement. A wave of talk ebbed from the front rows to the back.

"Good idea," said Nichols. "Let's vote on it."

The poll was taken, and Mordecai's move was approved unanimously.

"Very good," said Mordecai. "Now who wants to serve on this council?"

A breeze hummed through the pines. The miners waited apprehensively for one of their number to speak up. Faces turned nervously toward each other. Eyes shifted from side to side in search of volunteers. No one uttered a word.

"Come now, gentlemen," said Bemis. "This is America, where democracy prevails. Surely each and every one of you would like to hold office." There were no takers. "In that case, I offer my services to this community. I'd . . ."

"You'd do better by giving us better whiskey in your saloon," quipped a man in the rear.

"As I was saying," continued Bemis after the

laughter subsided. "I'd like to be a council member, Mr. Mayor."

"Very good, Mr. Bemis," said Mordecai. "Now we only need eight more."

"How about you, Mr. Nichols?" suggested Bemis.

Nichols straightened up at the suggestion.

"I'll second that," said Mordecai. "That makes two. Who else?"

"I'll serve," said McCatty.

"And me," said White.

"I'd like to withdraw," said Nichols after taking a moment to consider his nomination.

"It's too late for that," said Bemis. "You've already been named. Ain't that right, boys?"

A chorus of agreement followed.

"Then if elected," said Nichols, "I will not serve."

That merely drew laughs all around.

"On with the nominations," said Mordecai.

Five more men threw their names before the electorate, and Mordecai held the election. All were approved by a voice vote, and although Nichols remained adamant about withdrawing and not serving, his protestations, noticeably mild, went unheeded.

"Face it, Nichols," said Bemis after the meeting was concluded. "Duty calls."

"And it can keep calling," replied Nichols,

"because I don't intend to answer. I've got too much work to do now. I've got a mine to work."

"And now you have a constituency to serve," Bemis smiled.

CHAPTER 5

The mayor and the town council, of course, didn't constitute a legal government. The town would have to be chartered by the territorial legislature to make it official. For the meantime they would serve the purpose for which they were elected by the citizenry of Carthage City. Mordecai and the council could make all the laws they wished, but they were merely words as long as they didn't have someone to enforce them. That need was pointed out to the legislative group the day Pinky John Mallory arrived in town.

Gambling among mining men was as natural as eating and sleeping. Playing cards or rolling dice or spinning wheels were forms of relaxation after long days in the bowels of a mountain. None of the prospectors really took the games seriously.

Mallory was a man of a different ilk. He was

a professional, a leech who sucked gold from his victims who sat across from him at the tables. His real name was Sean Duncan Malloy, and he was a native of the Emerald Isle. He was brought to the United States as a baby in 1849. His father had made straight for the gold fields of California, never to be heard from again, leaving Sean's mother to provide for the infant in New York City. Growing up in the nation's largest city wasn't an easy task for a boy with an impoverished parent and a bad temper. He soon found himself on the wrong side of the law, and before he was more than a year into adolescence, Sean Malloy was a criminal wanted by the police. After killing an officer who had caught him robbing a drunken banker, Sean decided that he had best leave New York.

A former Confederate cavalry major named Charles Hollister Andrade took Malloy under his guidance and taught him the fine art of card playing. They plied their trade up and down the Mississippi, Ohio, and Missouri rivers until they had worn out their welcomes with a majority of the riverboat captains. They worked together as a team, taking a little here, a little there, but never too much from any single player or game.

When the waterways played out, the two

cardsharps discovered the cow towns of Kansas. The Texas boys who wound up weeks of hard trailing in places like Wichita, Salinas, and Fort Hays were quite willing to lose their pay to a pair of tinhorn gamblers as long as the game was kept clean. Things were going just fine for Malloy and his older partner until they decided to leave Kansas for the mining camps of Colorado. While crossing the Plains to Denver, the stagecoach they were riding was held up. Andrade refused to allow the outlaws to search him. He pushed one villain away from him, but a second would have none of that nonsense. He shot Andrade in the chest, and the game was finished.

Sean Malloy had by that time changed his name to John Mallory. He picked up his nickname in Denver while cleaning out a traveling jewelry salesman. After winning all the man's cash, Mallory permitted his opponent to bet two diamond rings. Needless to say, Mallory won the hand. When he tried on his winnings, he discovered that they would fit only his little fingers. He reasoned that that was as good a place as any to wear them, so the rings remained. Gradually, Mallory was given the nickname of Pinky John behind his back by those who disliked and mistrusted him. He learned about it from a stranger, and, oddly enough, he accepted it as flattery. The handle helped to enhance his reputation as a gambler and a killer. Few men would believe that a dude called Pinky John could handle a gun as well as a deck of cards. True nonbelievers were often laid to rest in the local boot hill.

Carthage City was celebrating a whole month of life when Pinky John rode into town. The street on both sides of Courtney Creek was well-worn and almost believable as a thoroughfare, thanks mostly to the constant traffic of horses, wagon wheels, and human feet. The pounding of carpenters' hammers and the buzzing of their saws alerted the traveler to the fact that Carthage City was passing from infancy to the toddler stage of its life.

A small dam had been built on Courtney Creek halfway down the mountainside. The stream continued to flow to the Gila River, but its course had been altered to run over a waterwheel, the source of power for a sawmill, which was supplying lumber for the builders. With materials available in bountiful supply, the carpenters and masons from Lordsburg and Silver City were quite busy erecting the city Mordecai Courtney envisioned.

Of course, the initial structure to be completed was the Courtney Building, simply because Mordecai had the funds to pay for it.

Bemis would have had his saloon up first, but it was a much larger job, what with it being two stories tall and requiring more skilled craftsmanship. A few houses, "shacks" according to the *Clarion*, were finished prior to the Courtney Building, but they didn't count by Mordecai's standards. A ten-by-ten wooden frame covered with slab wood and a slanted roof was hardly equal to the fifteen-by-thirty home of the newspaper.

In his weekly sheet Mordecai praised the work of the craftsmen as they hurried to construct each project. The fourth and fifth editions of the *Clarion* contained one article after another filled with descriptions of the work being done. It was Mordecai's intention that these stories should be read by folks in Lordsburg and Silver City, the two towns where Courtney also circulated his product. The *Clarion*, he knew, was the greatest instrument available for the continued promotion of Carthage City as a "Queen City of the West." The journalist had designs on making the town into something permanent, no matter whether the gold payed out or not.

To date there had been no signs of the yellow metal running out. Every day new strikes were being made. Piles of ore were beginning to rise outside a score of mines located on each side of the canyon. Jordan Waters, the assayer from Lordsburg, had moved into town to certify the quality of the rock being removed from the shafts, and from what he could determine there was an ample supply of gold in that particular section of the Burro Mountains.

Pinky John made mental notes of all his eyes could perceive as he passed up the street to George Bemis' Golden Palace Saloon. The Palace was still a tent with two planks laid across three beer kegs, but it did have a few tables with chairs and a wooden floor. Other than the furniture, the bar had no adorning features. Pinky John rather liked the simplicity of it as he entered and walked to the bar, where Bemis was wiping glasses.

"Afternoon, sir," greeted Bemis as he glanced up from his work. "What'll it be? Whiskey or cold beer?"

"Have you got a good Kentucky brand back of that bar?" asked Mallory.

"Ah, I see that you're a man of taste." Bemis smiled.

"I like to think so," said Mallory. He surveyed the room to find that he was alone with Bemis. "Not much of a crowd in here."

"Never is till after sundown." Bemis retrieved a shot glass and a bottle of Cumberland Gap Rye. "Will this do, sir?"

Mallory nodded after briefly inspecting the label. Bemis poured the customer a shot and watched him drink it down in a gulp. Bemis was taken with how Mallory held his little finger away from the glass as he drank, but he was more interested in the diamond ring on the digit. After another once-over, Bemis saw an identical ring on the same finger of the opposite hand.

"Another," said Mallory as he placed the glass on the counter.

"You know," said Bemis as he poured the second drink, "I once heard of a gambler who wore rings just like yours. I heard tell he was up in Denver not too long ago."

"I was," said Mallory, "but that was some time back. I haven't been there since '72. I've been to California a couple of times since then; Nevada, too. This is my first time down this way. I hope folks here are as friendly as they were in Virginia City."

"Now that all depends on how friendly you are, sir."

Mallory eyed Bemis, knowing fully what the saloonkeeper meant. It was time to strike the bargain. The gambler threw down the shot of whiskey, then placed the glass on the bar again for a final drink.

"No more than three for me," said Mallory.

"As much as I appreciate the taste of fine liquor, I don't indulge to any excess. Besides, I like to keep a clear head. You never know when you're going to need one."

"I wholeheartedly agree."

"John Mallory at your service, sir." He put forth a hand.

"George Bemis." He accepted the grip. "Word will get out quick that you're here, Mr. Mallory."

"I certainly hope it does. I've heard it told that men come from miles around to get a chance to play cards with Pinky John Mallory. It seems to me a foolish distance to travel just to part with your money."

"I take it you always win."

"Not always at cards," said Mallory.

"I see," said Bemis, "and where do you intend to set up your game?"

"I was hoping to use the rear of this establishment, providing of course that the price is right."

"I rent my tables for five dollars a day," said Bemis as he poured the third shot of whiskey into Mallory's glass. He reached for a second jigger and filled it with rye.

"I'm in the custom of giving my host a percentage of my winnings," said Mallory.

"But you said that you don't always win;

therefore, I'll take the five dollars and be happy. If you should do better, then that should be your good fortune. I don't take chances. A sure thing is my only wager."

"I can see that I'd better raise this glass to seal the bargain now or take leave of this place for good."

"You have a keen eye, Mr. Mallory," said Bemis as they completed the deal with the clinking of glass. The beverage was consumed in a gulp. "As a bonus, Mr. Mallory, I will supply the cards for your game. That way they can never be marked and my customers will have no room for complaint. The floor may be rough planks, but I would still dislike having blood spilled on it."

Mallory placed both hands on the bar. "These are for playing cards and self-defense. They don't go looking for trouble, but if it comes their way, they're ready to end it."

Bemis nodded. "When would you like to start?"

"Today would suit me," said Mallory as he dropped a $5 gold piece on the counter. "I'd like the table in the corner held for me each day until I give notice that I won't be needing it any longer."

Bemis reached beneath the bar and produced a pack of poker cards. "Agreed. I'll have a fresh deck waiting for you each day. I've got chips if you need them."

"I carry all the chips I need, and I have my own scale. My weights are in perfect order. I mention that in case you or anyone should want to inspect them or have them counterbalanced by some official of the law. I run an honest game, Mr. Bemis, and I expect everyone to deal with me in a like manner. I can tolerate being called a cheat. I won't draw down on a man simply because he can't hold his tongue, but if he makes a play, I'll end it for him."

"We haven't had any trouble in this town so far, Mr. Mallory, and I hope we never do. It's also my hope that it hasn't arrived in Carthage City with you."

"Like I said, Mr. Bemis, I won't start anything, but I will certainly bring it to a halt if trouble does come."

Bemis nodded his understanding. He slid the cards to Mallory, who picked them up and walked over to the table he had chosen for his game. The gambler sat down in the chair that was against the canvas wall. He plopped the deck unopened on the tabletop, took off his hat and placed it over the pack, then leaned back to wait for his first player.

As he busied himself with wiping glasses and

other chores about the bar, Bemis casually gazed at the street. From his vantage point he could see most of what transpired in Carthage City during the daylight hours. At that particular moment the only action of note was the labors of the carpenters and masons as they continued to erect Carthage City.

Later that day Bemis saw three men ride into town. They appeared to be cowboys. Their linen dusters, leather chaps, and coiled ropes on their saddles said they were men who punched cattle for a living. All three needed shaving, which told the average onlooker that they had been out on the range for a considerable period of time. High heels and deep arches on their boots were more firm evidence. Slowly, they rode to the saloon. They climbed down from their mounts like men with tired bones. As they peered about the town, they removed their chaps, gloves, and dusters. They tucked the hand apparel inside their belts and tied the overcoats and leather leg coverings to the saddles. Together they entered the bar.

Pinky John Mallory watched them cautiously as the three men strode up to the drinking counter. Bemis stepped over to them to take their orders.

"Is the beer cold?" asked the largest man, who stood in the middle.

"It's as cold as that stream outside can keep it," replied Bemis.

"That's good enough for me, barkeep. Set up a round." He tossed a quarter on the bar. "You ain't too busy this time of day, are you?"

"It's usually quiet in here till late afternoon," said Bemis as he drew three drafts. "Business starts picking up real good around sundown."

"I don't see no women around," said the stranger with a smile. "Too early for them?"

"We don't have any here yet," said Bemis as he brought the customers their drinks. "We will have some ladies up here in a few weeks if that's what you're interested in."

"We won't be here then."

"I see," said Bemis. "Are you here on business?"

"We're cattle dealers. My name is Ward, and these gents are my associates, Mr. Baker and Mr. Chester. We came up here wondering if we might find a butcher who was interested in buying some prime beef. We just bought a herd over by Roswell, and we're looking to unload it right away."

"We don't have a butcher here that I know of," said Bemis, "but we do have a storekeeper who might be interested in your stock. His name is Harry Willit. He's just returned from Silver City, so you should be able to find him in his shop across the street."

"We might look him up later," said Ward, "but for the moment I think we'll rest ourselves right here." He turned and looked at Mallory. "I see you got a gambling man here already. How's his game?"

"You'll have to find that out for yourselves," replied the saloonkeeper.

"Well, boys, how about it?"

"I could stand a hand or two," said Chester.

"Me, too," said Baker.

Mallory looked them over as they approached his table. The only curiosity he could see about them was the way they wore their sidearms. Each one had his holster slung low for quick action; hardly the fit a regular cowboy would use. The oddity escaped the scrutiny of Bemis.

"The barkeep says you got a game here," said Ward. "My friends and me got some ready cash. What's the limit?"

"Fifty cents to ten dollars," replied Mallory as he lifted his hat and pushed the sealed deck into the center of the table.

"Texas stud?" inquired Baker.

"If that's your game," said Mallory.

The three men sat down, and Mallory opened the pack of cards. He shuffled them several times, then offered the stack to Ward.

"High card deals the first hand," said the gambler.

Ward turned up an eight; Chester a king; and Baker a five. Each one was in the diamond suit. Pinky John's card was a five of spades. Chester reshuffled once, then offered the cards to Ward, who cut them. Four cards, one to each player, were dealt facedown, followed by four faceup. Chester caught a jack of spades for the high hand. He bet a dollar because he had an ace of spades in the hole. The others called his bet, and he dealt the next round. Ward became the new high with an ace of clubs, which paired the ace he had down. He tossed in two silver cartwheels, as did Chester and Mallory. Baker folded. After three more cards were displayed, Ward was still high. Confidently, he increased his wager to five dollars. Chester called and Mallory threw in. There was no sense in wasting any more money on that hand since a black three had broken the gambler's attempt at a heart flush. Ward and Chester played out the hand, and the bigger man won with his aces.

"Well, this looks like my lucky day," Ward grinned, showing a full set of tobacco-stained teeth. "Deal them up, gambling man. I can use a few extra bucks."

Mallory started the next hand. Baker

dropped out on the second card up. Ward had a pair of sevens showing on the third, which forced Mallory to withdraw. Chester paired queens on the last card and won the pot.

"You're not having much luck, are you, gambling man?" chuckled Chester.

"The game's just begun, gents," said Mallory.

Baker dealt the third round, and this time Mallory won with a pair of aces. The deal passed to Ward, and the three cattle dealers were quiet.

Seven of the next ten hands were won by Mallory, which aroused the anger of his opponents. Only a blind man would have missed the black looks Pinky John was receiving. To show his contempt for his unworthy adversaries, Mallory occupied both his hands by taking a cheroot from an inside coat pocket and lighting it slowly. The ploy served its purpose.

"I've lost enough," said Baker, who hadn't won a single pot. He pushed himself away from the table and sauntered over to the bar. "Another beer."

"Deal them out, gambling man," grunted Ward.

The game continued. Mallory dealt himself another winner, and Ward snatched up the cards in frustration. Chester took the next pot and the deal. Mallory won again, but Chester won the majority of the ten hands that followed, the others going Mallory's way. When Ward finished second best for the thirteenth consecutive time, he decided he'd had enough.

"You're awful lucky, gambling man," growled Ward.

Mallory glanced up from shuffling. "The name is John Mallory, Mr. Ward, and I wish you'd remember it."

"Pinky John Mallory?" gasped Chester.

"That's right."

"No wonder I've been losing," said Ward.

"Yeah," said Baker from where he was standing at the bar, "and that explains why I never won a hand."

"Yeah," agreed Ward.

"Hold on, gents," said George Bemis from behind the counter, a cocked Winchester held firmly in his hands and aimed at Ward's head. "I've seen a lot of card playing in my saloons, and I can spot a cheat across a smoke-filled room. Mr. Mallory has been playing you fair and square. You have no complaint with him."

"So you're in this together," accused Ward. "Well, we'll just see about this." He raised his hands above his shoulders and slid himself away from the table. "You've got the drop on me now, Mallory, but your time will come."

"Anytime you want to call the play," said Mallory.

"Not yet," said Ward, "but soon. You can bet on that, gambling man." He stood and kicked the chair away. "Let's get out of here, boys."

Chester gathered up his money as well as the few dollars that Ward had left on the table. He clearly displayed his hands full of coins as he followed his friend. Baker kept his hands away from him as he also walked toward the doorway. Each of them walked backward. Bemis maintained a bead on Ward until all three were outside. Mallory sat calmly at the table.

What none of the five men in the saloon saw was Mordecai Courtney riding back into town. He tied his horse to the rail in front of the *Clarion* and ran up the street to the foot bridge across Courtney Creek. He took the plank structure in three strides and made straight for the saloon, totally ignoring the three men who were then exiting the large tent. Quite unintentionally, the newspaperman bumped into Chester, who was just then turning around to face the street. Coins spilled everywhere.

"I'm terribly sorry," said Mordecai as he stooped to retrieve the man's money for him.

The distraction forced Ward's play. He dropped to a knee and went for his gun simultaneously. Baker drew and stepped to one side.

Chester pushed Mordecai to the ground and reached for his six-shooter.

The Winchester spat the first bullet, missing Ward by an instant. Pinky John Mallory ducked beneath the table where he was sitting. He cleared leather in a second and fired a quick round at Baker.

Mordecai's immediate reaction to the rough treatment he received was to complain verbally, but the first crack of gunpowder exploding paralyzed his tongue and forced him to hug the earth for his life.

Shots from the Colts of the three cowboys sprayed about the saloon, harming only glass and canvas. Bemis fired again at Ward, this time with the result of lead ripping through the meaty portion of the target's left shoulder.

"I'm hit!" screamed Ward as he reeled backward.

Baker turned to look at his friend, but the movement was his downfall. Mallory took advantage of the motion, which allowed him the heartbeat necessary for taking an accurate aim at Baker's chest. The .45-caliber slug from the gambler's Colt splintered a rib and tore through its victim's heart before leaving a ragged hole in the man's back. Baker tumbled to the street as he clutched at his breast.

Seeing one of his companions dead and the

other wounded, Chester thought to run, but the saloonkeeper's deadly rifle dropped him where he was kneeling as its third shot cracked his skull above the left eye.

Ward continued to fire at Mallory, but his aim was poor. As he pulled the trigger for the fifth time, a blast from Pinky John's revolver caught the wounded man in the throat. Ward crumpled next to the dead Baker.

As quickly as the fight had begun, it was finished. The three men who had said that they were cattle buyers lay dead at the entrance to the saloon. As quiet returned, Mordecai peeked up from the ground. Mallory came to his feet and approached the bodies with caution. Bemis did likewise.

"George, what happened?" asked Mordecai.

"It's all over, Mordecai," said Bemis.

The journalist awkwardly pulled himself into an upright position. With amazed eyes he viewed the gore.

"My God!" he swore. "Next time I'll watch where I'm going."

CHAPTER 6

Every miner in the vicinity heard the gunfire from the Golden Palace. The frequency and number of shots spurred the men to arm themselves and hurry into town.

Russ Nichols was among the last to arrive at the scene of the carnage. A crowd was gathered in front of the saloon, and Nichols pushed his way through the throng to get a close look at the bodies of the three dead cowboys, which Bemis and Deke McCatty had neatly laid out – eyes left half open, hats off, hands over their bellies – for everyone to view. A quick glance at Pinky John Mallory, who was seated at his table in the rear of the establishment, told Nichols what had transpired.

"Did he get them all by himself?" Nichols asked Bemis, motioning toward the gambler with his head.

"They started it," explained Bemis, "but I

helped them out of this world. Mallory wasn't looking for trouble, but those fellows seemed bent on having it out after he won a few hands of poker from them."

"Did you say 'Mallory'?" asked Nichols.

"Pinky John himself," said Bemis.

"I've heard of him. Never known of a town that didn't have a sudden increase in the cemetery population after he'd been there for a while."

Mordecai seemed to materialize from the cracks in the wooden floor of the barroom as he joined Nichols and Bemis. The journalist was clearly shaken by the bloody deaths. His face was paler than normal, and his breathing was rapid. A light glaze glistened between his wide eyelids.

"This is horrible," mumbled Mordecai.

Nichols looked down at his friend. "First time you've ever seen anything like this, Mordecai?"

"Simply horrible," he repeated.

Bemis put a hand on Mordecai's shoulder. "Easy, Mordecai. Maybe you should have a drink. Step up to the bar and have one on the house."

"Just horrible," said Mordecai, his stare fixed on the corpses.

Without warning or provocation, the big

prospector slapped the newspaperman across the cheek with an open palm. Although he tried to make it a gentle blow, Nichols knocked Courtney to the ground. He reached down to help his friend to his feet again.

"You needed that," said Nichols. "I didn't hurt you, did I?"

Mordecai brushed himself free of dust. "I'm not sure if I should thank you, Russ, although I can see your purpose in striking me in such a manner. No, I'm not hurt."

"A drink would have served the same purpose," said Bemis.

"Maybe so," said Nichols, "but one drink might have led to more. Our little friend needs a clear head for what we have to do today."

"What would that be?" asked Mordecai.

"We have to have a town meeting," said Nichols.

"What for?"

"For him." Nichols nodded in Mallory's direction. "That man has made it clear that we need a lawman in this town."

"I see," said Mordecai.

Bemis closed the Palace while the town council met to discuss the need Nichols had mentioned. Mordecai called the gathering to order and made it known why they were there.

"Gentlemen," began Mordecai, "if we are

to have a stable community here, we have to have law and order. We can't let another incident like the one that happened today happen again. Carthage City needs a marshal."

"Aw, come on, Mordecai," groaned Deke McCatty. "Getting a marshal in here isn't going to stop that sort of thing from happening again."

"Maybe so," said Frank White, "but a marshal can sure keep it from happening too often."

"I agree," said Nichols. "A marshal could do a lot to keep the peace in this town. Expecting one man to stop all the shootings by himself is asking too much, but if we get the right man for the job, he can do a lot to discourage men like Mallory from stirring up more trouble."

"Speaking of Mallory," said McCatty, "what are we going to do about him?"

"Let's send him on his way," said White.

"He hasn't broken any laws," said Bemis.

"He killed three men," retorted White.

"I killed one of them. Are you going to run me out of town, too?"

"Well, no," mumbled White.

"Then why should we run Mallory out of town?"

"Because a man like him draws trouble wherever he goes," said Nichols. "He's a bad penny, and you know it, George."

"Gentlemen," interrupted Mordecai, "as long as a man obeys the law, we have no reason nor the right to force him to leave Carthage City."

"I still don't like him or his kind being here," said Nichols. "Something has to be done about Mallory."

"I think we should leave that matter to our esteemed newspaper publisher," suggested Bemis. "I'm sure a few well-chosen words in print can give Mallory the hint he needs." Bemis really knew better, but he had to make a ploy that would pacify Nichols.

Mordecai stroked his chin with thumb and fingers. "I see what you mean, George. Just leave it to me. I'll let him know that we won't tolerate any further violence from him or his kind."

"Okay," said Nichols, "that's settled. Now what do we do about having a lawman?"

"Let's elect one," said Wilbur Hodge, a short bull of a man with a brown beard and bald head. Hodge's wit and sense of fair play made him popular with his fellows.

"Who do you know in Carthage City who can handle a gun properly?" asked Nichols.

Hodge gave it some thought before replying. "Well, George Bemis here is pretty fair with a gun."

A round of laughter followed the suggestion, but Hodge only half intended the remark to be taken lightly. Realizing he had succeeded, he withheld additional comment.

"I have a business to run," said Bemis. "What we need here is a real professional, a man with a solid reputation for upholding the law."

"Sounds to me like you know of such a man," probed Nichols.

"I've heard of one or two," reported Bemis. "The man I have in mind is Pete Spencer. The last I heard of him he was in Texas. He rode with the Rangers during the war, then punched cattle for a while. He got into a shoot-out up in Colorado back in '71 and killed two men. He went back to Texas and put on a badge for some little town near the Indian Territory. I once heard that he tracked two men for a whole winter through the Quachita Mountains. He finally cornered them in a cave near the Arkansas line. After nearly starving them to death, they came out shooting and he gunned them down. The town fired him because while he was gone the James gang robbed their bank. Last I heard about him he was riding herd for an outfit in the Panhandle."

"He sounds like the kind of man we want," said Nichols. "I say we send for him."

"I second that," said McCatty.

"All in favor?" asked Mordecai.

The decision was unanimous.

"Now this brings up another problem," said Nichols. "What are we going to do in the meantime?"

"We can be the law," said Bemis.

"How do you mean?" queried Mordecai.

"We can form a vigilance committee."

"I don't like the idea of mob rule," said Mordecai. "Mobs can be ugly and hard to handle. It's a bad way to mete justice."

"Maybe so," said Nichols, "but it's all we have until we can get Pete Spencer up here. I say we should form a vigilance committee right here and now. We're the town council, and that gives us the right."

"Are you willing to head up such a committee?" asked Bemis.

"I was thinking . . ."

"I think that's a good idea," said Hodge. "Russ Nichols for chairman of the vigilance committee."

"I second that motion," said McCatty.

"All in favor?"

"Wait a minute here," protested Nichols.

The other eight councilmen ignored their

colleague as they voiced their approval to the plan.

"The motion is carried," reported Mordecai. "Now what do we do about a committee?"

"We can all be the committee," suggested Bemis.

"All won't be necessary," said Hodge. "I think we can get by with three or four of us for the time being. What do you think, Russ?"

"So now you want my opinion. Well, I'd like to tell you what I really think, but they would be words wasted. Since you've all seen fit to put me in charge, I'll select my own committee. McCatty, White, and Hodge will be enough. If we need more, the rest of you fellows will be available. Agreed?"

The flint in the prospector's eyes said that there had better not be any dissenting votes. The plan was accepted without further argument.

When the meeting broke up and the Palace was reopened for business, all but Nichols and Mordecai stayed for drinks on the house. Nichols repaired to his campsite, and Mordecai returned to the Courtney Building to write the story about the shooting in the saloon. After penning the article, he turned to the task of editorializing on the fatal occasion. Without mincing words, he scalded the violent act as well as its major participant. Seeing that George Bemis was a friend, advertiser, and subscriber who was merely protecting his property, Mordecai saw no reason to include the owner of the Golden Palace in the caustic attack.

By the following evening the citizenry of Carthage City had read the latest edition of the *Clarion*, and with but a single exception it was well received. The miners and businessmen were delighted over the results of the town council meeting, and they were equally happy about the position which the newspaper had taken on violence and violent men.

The single dissenter in the populace was, of course, Pinky John Mallory. For some odd reason, he was offended by such phrases as "despicable bloodletter" and "undesirable element." The crowning insult was the insinuation that Mallory had provoked the gunfight by being too expert at his trade. And, of course, there was no mention of how Mordecai had precipitated the gore of bullets and blood by stumbling into the saloon at the most inopportune moment.

If the article and editorial had been all the punishment Mallory was forced to endure, the gambler could have overlooked the provocation by the diminutive editor.

Unfortunately for all parties concerned, Mallory was the object of derision and the point of humor throughout the town. He took the brunt of the sarcastic remarks fostered by Mordecai's poignant prose with an apparent deaf ear, but when Deke McCatty entered the Golden Palace and sat down at Mallory's table, Pinky John reached the limit of his tolerance.

"You still here?" asked McCatty in the way of a greeting.

Mallory's eyes were cold and penetrating, but his lips were silent to the inference.

"My game is still open," said Mallory.

"Why? There ain't no one going to be playing poker with you ever again. Least ways, not in this town. I would have thought you to be smarter, Mallory. Can't you see that you're not wanted here any longer?"

"What are you accusing me of?" demanded the gambler.

McCatty placed both of his hands flat on the table, sweat beading on his forehead. The action, or lack of it, said that he was unarmed and wasn't looking for a fight.

"I only know what I read in the paper," replied McCatty, sidestepping the issue.

Mallory's head bobbed silently a few times. "I see. Excuse me, friend, but I have some business to attend to."

The sun was close to the horizon when Mallory stepped outside the Golden Palace. He scanned both ends of the street for something or someone. Whatever it was he wanted to see wasn't on his side of Courtney Creek, so he headed for the foot bridge opposite Willit's store. Once he was across the wooden structure, he turned left toward the Courtney Building.

Mordecai dropped the last double eagle into his secret cashbox and closed the cover. With the suspicious view of an Ebenezer Scrooge, his eyes scoured the room for a set of peeking orbs. Satisfied that no one was watching him, he hid the tin container beneath the tray of type next to the press. Feeling his fortune was safe for the night, the journalist slipped into his frock coat and new bowler and moved for the front door to the establishment. Stepping through it, he reached into a trouser pocket for the key. As he turned it in the lock, he heard his name called by an unfamiliar voice.

"I want to talk to you, Courtney," said Pinky John as he approached Mordecai from the street.

The newspaperman straightened to his full height of five feet one and a half inches. The shadow over Mallory's face warned him that the meeting was going to be less than friendly.

His instincts told him to run, but the stubborn streak that dominated most of his actions stayed his feet.

"Speak your piece, Mallory, and be quick about it. I have a thirst to quench and a stomach to fill, and I'm anxious to be about that business."

"You had plenty of time to write that tripe about me in your newspaper. I should think you could give me a moment to rebut the inaccuracies you printed in that rag."

"When and if I should ever print anything that is inaccurate, I will gladly print a retraction to rectify the mistake."

"I'm glad to hear you say that," said Mallory, a lighter tone sparking his words. "About that editorial . . ."

"Oh, it's my editorial that you object to, is it? Well, sir, I'm sorry, but an opinion is simply that. Whatever my stand may be, I stick by it, no matter the feelings of others."

"Then you persist with your opinion that I am despicable?"

"I believe that was the word I used, yes."

"And you still believe that Carthage City is no place for me?"

"I see that you've grasped my very intention in the editorial," said Mordecai with a sadistic smile. He shouldn't have grinned.

A cornered animal is vicious, but a wounded beast with its back to a wall is lethal. Mallory was the latter, and Mordecai was too inexperienced in the ways of the West to know that he was confronting a grizzly bear with a twig.

Pinky John's Irish temper erupted with the fury of an angry Thor. His right hand, flat but as firm as an armored gauntlet, lashed out and crashed into the side of Mordecai's face and ear. The strength of the blow sprawled the smaller man in the dust.

"You little bastard!" spat Mallory. "You're the one who ought to be run out of town. You and that lying rag of yours!" Mallory's foot landed squarely on Mordecai's rump. "Damn you! I run an honest game, and I don't look for trouble. But you've made me out to be some sort of vermin that leeches off widows and orphans. Damn you!" Another kick kept Mordecai on the ground. "I ought to . . ."

"But you won't," interrupted Russ Nichols as he came up behind Mallory.

Mallory spun around to face the miner, simultaneously drawing his Colt. "Stay out of this," he growled.

"I'm not heeled," said Nichols, showing empty hands while holding his step. He eyed the gun. "Kill me and you'll be strung up for sure."

A crowd began to grow around the three men. Mordecai struggled to his feet and stumbled toward Nichols.

"Are you all right?" asked Nichols.

"None the worse for the wear."

"Okay, Mallory, you've had your revenge. Now leave this town tonight."

"I'll leave when I've a mind to leave," sneered the gambler.

The hammer of Deke McCatty's six-shooter clicked into place behind Mallory. Although he knew he could be shot in the back at any second, Pinky John felt the holder of the weapon was bluffing. Casually, he relaxed his grip on his own Colt and replaced it in the holster.

"I'm not afraid of you, Nichols, but murder isn't part of my game. If you want me out of town, you'll have to throw me out personally. I won't go without a fight."

"Don't trust him, Russ," cautioned Mordecai.

"I've got the drop on him, Russ," said McCatty. "Just say the word and I'll see that he leaves one way or another."

"Put your gun away, Deke," said Nichols. "I can handle this tinhorn."

"I'll take off my gun, Nichols," said Mallory, "and we can settle this with our fists. You whip me and I'll leave. If not, I stay and go about my business. Fair enough?"

"You don't have to fight him, Russ," said Mordecai.

"Take off that gun belt, Mallory," commanded Nichols.

Pinky John smiled as he complied.

"Fight!" someone yelled for the whole town to hear, which wasn't really necessary because a majority of the citizens were already gathered around the antagonists. The men spread out to form a human ring, and before the first punch was thrown they called out encouragements to Nichols to do a real job on the fancy dude.

Casually, Mallory removed his coat and hung it on the rail in front of Mordecai's office. He was confident that he could take the big miner. He had fought several times and had the advantage of experience as well as the knowledge of self-defense, which he had learned from a professional prizefighter while plying his trade on the Mississippi. He quickly took a pugilist's stance and approached Nichols.

George Bemis stepped to the front of the crowd. Recognizing the prowess which Mallory displayed with his maneuvering, he saw that although Nichols was the larger and obviously stronger man Pinky John was an equal if not superior match.

"Any bets, gents?" queried Bemis.

"You taking Mallory?" asked Frank White.

"Even money?"

"How much?"

"I've got a hundred dollars," said Bemis.

"I'll take ten of that," said White.

As the two fighters continued to size up each other, other bettors chimed in, and Bemis had his wagers covered.

"Hold on," said Mallory before he and Nichols could begin the bout. "If there's going to be any gambling, I want in on it. Mr. Bemis, will you take all the money you need from my coat to cover any bets and hold them for me?"

"Will do," agreed Bemis.

Another round of betting ensued.

"Okay, gentlemen," said Bemis. "All bets are down. You may begin."

Mallory squared off. Nichols closed his fists and stalked his prey. A lightning left jabbed the miner twice in the face before he saw it coming. He blinked away the sting of the blows, thinking they were too light to have caused any damage, but the salty taste of blood inside his lower lip told him differently. He swung at Mallory in anger, but Pinky John ducked cleanly beneath the right. The gambler landed a combination to Nichols' midsection, and the prospector felt the air blast from his lungs, followed by the cramp of his diaphragm. Another series of lefts and then a strong right to his head rocked him backward. He stumbled and would have fallen had not some of the spectators caught him. He shook off the pain and charged his opponent. Mallory side-stepped and tripped Nichols with a trailing foot, sending him to the ground.

"Foul!" cried a man in the crowd.

"Women!" came a shout in the distance.

"Women?" queried a man on the fringe of the throng.

Nichols got to his feet and started after Mallory again. Expecting Pinky John to make the same move again, Nichols was slower with his approach. He swung wildly, and Mallory leaned away from the fist, which missed him by less than an inch. He countered with a hard right to the miner's chin, straightening him and stunning Nichols' senses.

"Women!" came the cry again.

A few heads turned to see Julius Heintz, the sawmill operator, running up the road from the valley. He was waving his hat over his head in an effort to draw attention to himself.

"Women!" he shouted again.

Mallory knocked Nichols to the ground a second time.

"Women!" shouted Heintz.

The word rippled through the men until it reached the innermost round. As the distraction overwhelmed the main attraction, the cheering ceased, and an anxious quiet settled over the onlookers, as well as the contestants, one standing and one on his knees.

"There's women coming up the road!" shouted the breathless Heintz.

The fight was forgotten. Queer, puzzled looks were exchanged from man to man and then to the approaching Heintz.

"Women, I tell you!"

"Women?" mumbled half the men.

"WOMEN!" roared the remainder.

CHAPTER 7

They were early but no one in Carthage City cared. They were women, and that was what the all-male population of the town wanted. It made little difference that they were dance-hall girls who would hustle them for drinks and sing an occasional song. They were soft, sweet-smelling, and wore dresses instead of pants.

Sarah Macomb, nicknamed Louisiana Sal, her flaming red hair wafted by the breeze, was the first to step out of the coach. She held a straw bonnet in one hand as George Bemis helped her down. The rustle of her long purple dress stirred the moonlight imaginations of all the men gathered around the chartered stage-coach. The excitement of the previous minutes was now a thing of ancient recollection.

"How you doing, Georgie?" asked Sarah as she smiled at Bemis.

"Glad to see you, Sal." The saloonkeeper

beamed. He turned to the crowd, which included Mallory and a groggy Nichols, their fight concluded for the moment. "Men, this is Louisiana Sal."

"Hiya, boys!" she greeted the gaping throng. "Meet my girls!"

One by one, five young women emerged from the carrier. The first was a mulatto, the daughter of a black slave and a Creole plantation owner from near Baton Rouge. The next was Chinese, a girl whose parents had sold her to a traveling salesman who then lost her to Louisiana Sal Macomb in a poker game. Third to step down was the daughter of a French sea captain and a Mexican prostitute. The last two ladies were twins, orphaned by Yankee guns when Farragut bombarded Mobile.

All of them were dressed in dark-green cotton dresses with white collars and cuffs. With their wide-brimmed sun hats, they looked more like five graduates of a finishing school than dancehall girls. Other than their attire, the greatest common denominator they shared was their love for the boss, Louisiana Sal, who was more their mother than their employer. Sal had taught them everything from the 3-Rs to how to handle a drunk. She kept them out of trouble and kept trouble away from them. They were her girls, and she was their boss. It was an arrangement which suited them all.

Like each of her charges, Sal had a tale of her own.

Her father had emigrated to America from Scotland in 1844. When the Mexican War broke out, he enlisted in the U.S. Army and was sent to New Orleans as a powder monkey in a gunnery crew that manned the big cannons which guarded the port. Graham Macomb met Cornelia Witherspoon while on liberty in the city, and although his intentions were always quite honorable, their union was forbidden by Sal's maternal grandfather, a wealthy cotton exporter. As young lovers sometimes do when their desire is blocked, the couple married secretly. When the clandestine wedlock became known to him, Sal's grandfather was enraged. He tried to have the marriage annulled but couldn't because Cornelia was with child. The old man then did what he considered to be the next best thing. With a bribe in the right place, he had Graham transferred to a post in Kansas.

Graham Macomb died of pneumonia the following winter, never knowing that his wife had given birth to his daughter.

Cornelia Macomb, uninformed that her husband was deceased, left New Orleans with her month-old child in an attempt to join him.

Weakened by the ordeal of giving birth, she contracted a consumptive cough on the riverboat passage to St. Louis. Knowing she was penniless, the captain of the ship paid a doctor to treat her and asked Alice Rankin, a friend and the madame of a riverfront brothel, to keep watch on both physician and patient.

The lady of ill repute grew close to Cornelia in her last days and promised the dying mother that she would see to it that baby Sarah was placed in her father's custody. When it was learned that Graham had also passed away, Alice Rankin located Sarah's grandfather and asked him to take the infant, but he refused, saying that he had disowned his daughter and therefore would have nothing to do with any offspring of hers. Alice, although feeling herself unfit to do so, became Sarah's only family.

Even though she raised Sarah in a bordello, Alice Rankin managed to separate her young charge from her professional life. Bit by bit, however, Sarah learned why men visited the house, and when she asked Alice about it, her foster-mother told her the truth but at the same time exacted a promise from Sarah that she would never, under any circumstance, take up the trade.

At the outbreak of the War Between the States, Alice Rankin died from injuries received in a carriage accident, leaving all her worldly possessions, which included the ownership of the business, to Sarah. Only fourteen at the time, a guardian was appointed by the court for Sarah, but the teen-ager felt she didn't need anyone to look after her any longer. Taking the jewels and cash Alice had left her, she ran away to New Orleans, hoping to find any family of hers that might be left there.

When none of her relatives would admit the blood between them, Sarah almost turned to the only life she knew, but the vow she had given Alice haunted her into avoiding it at all costs. Instead, she became a dancer and singer in a minstrel show. That job led her to Mobile, where she found the twins. Remembering the love Alice Rankin had given her, an orphan, Sarah thought the best way to return the affection was to share herself with Elizabeth and Victoria.

Discovering how lonely men would pay as much to watch women dancing and hear them sing as they would for other favors, Sarah formed her own show and took it west. Several girls came to her and left her over the years, but none of them shamed her by breaking the promise she had given to Alice.

There were lots of towns in the West, but the booming new mining centers held the most money. As she scanned the faces of the men gawking at her and the five young ladies with her, Louisiana Sal Macomb wondered how much of that wealth she could glean in Carthage City.

In the same order in which they had lighted from the coach, Sal introduced her troupe to the men of Carthage City.

"Boys, this is Jeanette, Joy, Maria, Elizabeth, and Victoria. I know you're going to like them all." Turning to Bemis, she asked, "Where's your saloon, Georgie?"

"Over there, Sal," said Bemis, pointing to the incomplete structure that would be the permanent home of the Golden Palace Hotel and Saloon.

"It's not done yet."

"Well, I wasn't expecting you so soon."

"Well, we're here, and we aren't leaving. But we're not going to open the show until that place is finished."

"But, Sal . . ."

"No buts about it, Georgie. We don't dance in tents, and that's all there is to it. If you want us to work, you get that saloon finished."

"You heard her, men," announced Bemis. "There will be no show until my saloon is finished."

The miners groaned collectively.

"Well?" spoke up Deke McCatty. "What are we waiting for? Let's get the place built."

Just as they had worked to complete the road up from the valley, the miners helped the carpenters and masons on the Golden Palace. Within three days and nights the building was open for business, and Louisiana Sal and her girls were rehearsing on the small stage in the rear of the barroom.

The dispute between Pinky John Mallory and Russ Nichols was temporarily set aside but not forgotten. The fight had been declared a draw by George Bemis, even though he had thought Mallory would have won had it been fought to a conclusion. The men who had placed wagers with him might have agreed but were glad that he had the decency to return their moneys to them.

Mallory was also willing to let the bettors have their ways. Like Bemis, he felt he could have given Nichols a thrashing, but as he reviewed the events of the day, he was correct in assuming that Louisiana Sal and her ladies had arrived in Carthage City at the most opportune time. For had he beaten the big miner, the others, in their wrath over losing their dollars, might have seen fit to lynch him. That thought alone convinced him that a draw had been the better outcome.

Surprisingly, Russ Nichols held the same feeling as Mallory. As much as he disliked the gambler, he found a new respect for the man. Any dude who could throw punches the way Mallory did deserved certain considerations, and Russ Nichols always gave a fellow his just dues. Besides, Mordecai had been a little unfair to Pinky John in the editorial.

A posterior bruise, the result of Pinky John's well-placed foot movement, reminded Mordecai for the next few days of the near beating he had suffered. The incident did serve to reinforce the fact that he was currently residing in the West, where men often spoke with their fists and guns before choosing the more civilized method of communication. After several minutes of debate with himself, Mordecai decided that he would be wise to adopt the custom of the West.

"I'd like to look at some handguns," said Mordecai as he stood at the counter in Harry Willit's store.

"Guns, Mordecai?" quizzed the astonished storekeeper.

"That's right, Harry," replied Mordecai. "And something to carry one in. A holster I can wear rather inconspicuously."

Willit shook his head once, then retrieved a tray of six-shooters from its place beneath the glass case. He placed the weapons on the cabinet top for Mordecai's inspection.

"Take your pick," said Willit.

The usual customer would have done just that, gripping the first that attracted his attention, hefting it, sighting it, spinning the chamber, thumbing the hammer, making a complete examination of the death dealer. Mordecai's only move was to shove his hands into his pants pockets, and like a small boy peering wistfully into a jar of hard candies, he remained motionless, wide-eyed, and staring. The difference was Mordecai wasn't wishing for a sample. The sight of the dead cowboys, their blood drying in the sun on their lifeless corpses and the flies buzzing around them, excogitated in his brain, prompting him to recall the extreme distaste he held for violence. The lumbar muscles in his back tightened and wrenched him with a spasm of pain, awakening him from the triple phantasm which horrified him so.

"Have you got anything smaller?" queried Mordecai. "You know, something more suitable for me."

"I don't carry derringers, if that's what you're looking for." Willit studied Mordecai briefly. "But I do have a four-shot pistol that you might like."

The storekeeper bent over and opened a drawer beneath the display case. Upright again, he held out a .25-caliber Remington revolver, chrome- and nickel-plated with an ivory handle.

"I bought this from a traveling gunsmith who was down on his luck," explained Willit. "I've never had any use for it, so you might as well have it."

Mordecai's eyes brightened as he reached for the gun. "Pretty, isn't it? And it's just the right size for me." He looked up at Willit. "How much, Harry?"

"For you, Mordecai" – Willit smiled – "just twenty dollars, and I'll throw in a box of shells. Might as well. I don't get any call for them."

"Has it got a holster?"

"No, but I can have one made for you."

"Well, I'd like to wear it on the left side," said Mordecai. He touched his waistline to indicate the spot where he wanted the gun holder. "You know, I'm right-handed, and I'd like to reach across my gut to draw."

"I see what you mean. I'll have it made that way."

"Good. In the meantime, I'll just tuck it inside my pants." Mordecai beamed at the pistol. "I can't wait to try it."

"Not on anyone we know, I hope." Willit frowned.

"No, of course not, Harry. I just want to practice on some cans and bottles. I hope I never have to use it on another human being."

"I feel the same way."

Mordecai reached into a trouser pocket, pulled out a double eagle, and presented it to the merchant.

"Are you going over to the Palace tonight, Harry?"

"I wouldn't be if my wife was here" — Willit smiled — "but seeing as she's still in Silver City, I'll be there in a front-row seat."

"Maybe we can share a table?" suggested Mordecai. "The first drink will be on me."

"You've got a deal. See you tonight, Mordecai."

The journalist nodded and slid the Remington inside his waistband. With a little wave of farewell, he left the store.

For the first time in his adult life, Mordecai Courtney felt he was equal in stature to any man. He patted the bulge on his left side, then started down the street toward his office. To the casual observer, he appeared to be stepping like a bantam rooster who had just become cock-o'-the-walk. The confidence which buoyed him was only a hollow assurance brought on by the weight of the four-shot revolver. The elation would wear off soon enough.

As he neared the Courtney Building, Mordecai's attention was drawn to the presence of a stranger loitering about the front door. Immediately, the journalist recognized him as a man of means and probably great importance. A little less than average height, portly, and apparently approaching his twilight years, the gentleman was perfectly groomed and attired. Salty sideburns matched a bushy mustache that was free of wax. A derby hid the remainder of his hair. Mordecai noted that the man wore spats under the trousers of his navy-blue, gold-pinstriped suit. A solid-gold watch chain was hanging leisurely across the front of the matching vest. Yes, thought Mordecai, this person represented wealth.

"Good day, sir," said the visitor, tipping his hat with one hand and offering to shake with the other. Mordecai accepted the greeting. "Are you the proprietor of this establishment?"

"Yes, indeed, sir, I am. Mordecai Courtney at your service."

"I'm glad to make your acquaintance, Mr. Courtney. Beecher Hay is my name. I'm vice president of Southwest Arizona Mining Company."

Mordecai had never heard of the outfit, but he wasn't going to tell Hay that.

"Indeed, sir. Welcome to Carthage City. What brings you to our fair town? Business or pleasure?"

"A fair town it is from what I've seen thus far," said Hay, avoiding the question. "And prosperous, I might add."

"It certainly is that, Mr. Hay." A sudden recollection of etiquette forged its way into Mordecai's brain. "Would you care to step into my office where we can be seated?"

Hay stroked a hip. "Inside, yes, but as for sitting, I'm rather reluctant. You see, I traveled up here by the roughest of means."

"Horseback?" inquired Mordecai.

"Precisely, a conveyance which I am unaccustomed to using with any frequency."

"Yes, the saddle can be torturous when one isn't in the habit of riding," said Mordecai with a sly smile. "Excuse the mild pun, sir."

"Think nothing of it, Mr. Courtney. I rather enjoy the turn of a witty word. I should suspect that you must do that quite often in your profession."

"Indeed, sir," said Mordecai. He removed the key from a pocket and unlocked the door. With a wave of a hand, he bid Hay enter the premises, then followed him inside. "Please

115

take a chair, sir."

Hay sat down gingerly on a straight-back that was hewn from a local pine. Although crude, it was sturdy and more comfortable than it appeared to be. Mordecai hung his bowler on the hat tree in the corner and scurried around to the wooden armchair behind his cluttered desk. When he sat, the butt of the Remington gouged into his midsection. He winced but imperceptibly. A quick hand maneuver pushed it into a more satisfactory position.

"To answer your question previous," said Hay, "I've come to Carthage City to determine whether there is sufficient ore here for a major mining operation, an endeavor my company would certainly enjoy entertaining."

"Indeed, sir," said Mordecai with raised eyebrows. He took up a pencil and found a blank sheet of writing paper for note-taking. "I hope you don't object, but it is the nature of my profession to record the newsworthy."

"Of course," said Hay. "Precisely the reason I've come to you first. A town's newspaper publisher usually knows everything that is happening within his locality."

"An astute deduction."

"As I was saying, Southwest is always interested in new finds, but not all prove to be deserving of our efforts. When a strike does present itself meritorious, we locate a stamp mill in the vicinity. That is my purpose in being here. It is my duty to make such a determination as to the feasibility of that sort of project."

"Well, we certainly have several men removing ore of high quality from the surrounding slopes. At last count, twenty-three mines were producing high-grade rock. Our local assayer, Mr. Jordan Waters, has reckoned that there is ample reason for optimism in this area."

"Really now. I'm quite impressed by this sort of talk. I'd like to speak with this man Waters and, of course, the owners of the producing mines. Do you think this could be arranged?"

"Certainly, sir. It would be my pleasure to call a meeting of the miners. Anything which helps the growth of this community is a pleasure to me."

Hay's voice went conspiratorial. "A word of caution, Mr. Courtney. I'm not making any promises. I won't be making any decisions until after my own engineer has had the opportunity to survey everything. We at Southwest are known for our thoroughness."

"So I've heard, sir," lied Mordecai. "One thing, Mr. Hay, I might request of you in reciprocation. Would you please withhold your identity until I've had the chance to announce your arrival in my newspaper?"

"When will your next edition be out, Mr. Courtney?"

"Tomorrow."

"I don't see that it would be an inconvenience for me," agreed Hay. "Good relations with the local newspaper are often essential in the mining industry. I'll simply keep my position with Southwest a secret until you've made the proper announcement. In the meantime, could you recommend an establishment where I might find food and refreshment as well as a room and a bath?"

"The Golden Palace should fill your needs, Mr. Hay, and if you're looking for entertainment, Miss Sarah Macomb and her dancing belles will be opening their act tonight. If you care to join me, I have a table in the front, and one chair is yet unspoken for."

"Miss Sarah Macomb, you say?"

"That's correct. Do you know her?"

"I had occasion to meet her in New Orleans some years ago," said Hay. "I doubt that she'll recall the introduction. No matter. I graciously accept your invitation." Hay rose to leave. He proffered another handshake. "Until this evening then?"

"Good day, sir." Mordecai smiled.

As soon as Hay was absent from the office,

Mordecai set about getting out the next number of the *Clarion*. The lead story had been about the arrival of Louisiana Sal and her troupe, but Mordecai thought it would serve the interests of the town if he placed the article concerning the mining executive at the top of the front page. True to his word, Mordecai stated in the paper that Hay had come to Carthage City only to make an inspection of the diggings and was not necessarily in a buying mood. To enhance the single page, he also ran an item about the virtues of Carthage City as possibly becoming the new hub of the mining industry in New Mexico Territory. A little promotion, he reasoned, never hurt when you're trying to build a stable community, and that was exactly what Mordecai was attempting.

CHAPTER 8

The new Golden Palace Hotel and Saloon, Geo. Bemis, Esq., Proprietor, was an outstanding accomplishment. To be sure, the architecture was nothing unique; it was basic western whiskey mill. And it wasn't the only jughouse in town. To the contrary, the Palace was only one of nine watering holes in Carthage City.

The dissimilarity between the Palace and its counterparts stemmed from its owner, George Bemis. His experience behind the bar entitled him to the designation of mixologist, whereas his contemporaries were mere bardogs serving up straight liquor and warm beer. He could expertly mix a Bloody Mary or an extra dry martini as well as a variety of cobblers, slings, juleps, sours, sangarees, and toddies. Moreover, Bemis had the ingredients for almost any concoction a man with a thirst might want at any time of the day or night.

But far above his expertise with a mixing tumbler, Bemis possessed the all-important factor which placed him ahead of the other saloonkeepers. He had the capital which was necessary to erect an establishment such as the Golden Palace. Over the years he had spent toiling for other owners, Bemis had wisely saved his money, watching for the day when the right town would spring up where he could build for himself. When news of Carthage City's birth reached him, he saw the opportunity to strike out on his own, and being the first man in the business of selling alcoholic beverages to arrive in the fledgling village, he was able to purchase the choicest lot for the fine structure he had envisioned during the slow days and nights working for someone else.

With the availability of good pine from the sawmill of Julius Heintz, constructing the walls and roof of the Golden Palace was an easy task, but the furnishings and other adornments, such as lamps, mirrors, glass windows, and a full-length bar, had to be freighted in from the railroad depot at Lordsburg. And, of course, all those items had to be transported from points east. Bemis was fortunate in that his orders were expedited quickly, and delivery was completed long before the house was ready to serve its first thirsty customer.

The finished Golden Palace Hotel and Saloon had two entrances in its sixty-foot front: one with double doors complete with long rectangular glass panes for the hotel portion and the other with two sets of hinged portals — the outer similar to those aforementioned and the inner a pair of swinging gates — leading into the saloon. The hotel lobby was a square room with a clerk's desk, mailboxes behind it, two cushioned chairs, a stairway leading up to the rooms, and a doorway to the bar. A four-lamper was suspended from the ceiling to provide light at night, and two windows, one in the front wall and the other in the side at the foot of the staircase, illuminated the room during the daylight hours.

At the top of the stairs a hall crossed the width of the building to another set of steps which led down to the saloon. Intersecting the passageway was another which ran the length of the structure. At each end were doors to the outside: one to the back stairs and the other to the balcony, which reached out over the street. The hotel's fourteen rooms were off this hallway. Each lodging contained a double bed, nightstand, and bureau of drawers with a pitcher and washbasin. All the floors were bare wood.

The barroom, which Bemis christened "The

Bonanza Room," received all of the owner's attention to ornament. The bar was, of course, his masterpiece. Created from imported Circassian walnut by Brunswick of Chicago, it was the *ne plus ultra* of drinking counters. A brass footrail ran its length of fifty-two feet. Four copper cuspidors were spaced evenly along the footrest. The mantel had pyramids of drinking glasses stacked on it, each interspaced by bottles of Old Crow, Chapin & Gore, Martel Brandy, Martel Cognac, White Seal Bordeaux, Virginia Reel Sipping Whiskey, Cumberland Rye, New Orleans Bourbon, Kentucky Bourbon, Tennessee Walker Scotch, Hang-dog Hooch, Jim Beam, Johnny Walker, Paris Burgundy, Rheinwein, Old Towse, and Denver Dynamite. Three barrels of Milwaukee and St. Louis lager were placed one at each end and one in the middle of the backbar. On the wall, a large mirror, flanked by two smaller ones at each side of it, reflected the images of the patrons. Beneath the bar, Bemis kept extra bottles, kegs of beer, a washbasin, and his Winchester.

At the rear of the hall, the stage protruded into the room. Two dozen tables, with four straight-back chairs around each, were organized in six rows of four. Toward the front was the gaming area, where Pinky John Mallory ran his poker game. Three wagon-wheel chandeliers hung down from the ceiling to provide some light throughout the day as well as the night. The windows on either side of the doors were frosted glass, which allowed little additional illumination from dawn to dusk, but they prevented anyone from seeing inside the establishment no matter what the time. The wall opposite the bar was decorated with four large paintings of desirable, scantily garbed ladies as they reclined on couches.

The Golden Palace was the exception instead of the rule as far as western saloons went. It had the class of a Denver or San Francisco bistro, and it also compared favorably with eastern taverns. George Bemis had built a lavish watering hole, and he was proud of it because he knew that it ranked as one of the finest in the whole territory. As he looked at the full house which had crowded in the opening of Louisiana Sal's show, he knew that he had done the right thing in bringing his business to Carthage City.

Mordecai was the last patron to enter the premises that evening, and when he did, Bemis announced his arrival and said the performance could begin. A cheer of approval went up from the hearty throats of the men. As the journalist found his way to the table Bemis had set aside for him, Mordecai noted that all three of his guests were there ahead of him.

"Good evening, gentlemen," said Mordecai as he seated himself. "Have you already introduced yourselves around?"

"We've met," said Russ Nichols. He gave Mordecai a hard look. "I have a bone to pick with you, Mordecai. Why didn't you tell me Mr. Hay was in town? I would have thought you would have been so excited that you couldn't wait to tell me of his arrival."

Mordecai looked to the mining executive questioningly.

"I'm certain Mr. Courtney has been too busy with his work to mention to anyone that a mere banker has come to Carthage City," said Hay with a smile. "Is that not so, Mr. Courtney?"

"Uh, yes, indeed it is, Mr. Hay," agreed Mordecai, relieved by Hay's tale.

"Prior to your arrival, Mr. Courtney," continued Hay, "I was telling Mr. Willit and Mr. Nichols how we had met this afternoon at your office and how we had discussed the need for a bank in Carthage City."

"Yes, we certainly do need a bank," concurred Mordecai.

Before the conversation could become more exaggerated, the tinny tones of a piano interrupted. All eyes were turned to the stage with great expectancy, and without further delay, Louisiana Sal and her girls appeared on the raised platform. Sal came out wearing a low-cut black satin dress trimmed in gold lace, while the dancers behind her wore outfits with shorter skirts that were colored just the opposite of the singer's. They performed three songs and high-kicking dances for the appreciative house before disappearing into the wings.

An agreement between Sarah Macomb and George Bemis had been concluded through the mails weeks prior to the dance-hall girls coming to Carthage City. The saloon proprietor agreed to provide the women with bed and board, and they would give three shows nightly in the Bonanza Room. The monetary portion of the contract said the girls would circulate among the customers between performances asking the men to buy them drinks. Instead of liquor, Bemis would serve the ladies tea, but the price would be the same as for the hard stuff. Bemis would then split fifty-fifty with the women at the end of the business day. It was an equitable arrangement for all but the man on the receiving end of the bar.

Like a mother hen, Louisiana Sal led her charges into the barroom. They fanned out in all directions, but Sal headed straight for Mordecai's table. On the way, Deke McCatty

126

grabbed her around the waist and pulled her down on his lap. From the odor of his breath, Sal could tell that he was already several drinks toward putting on a heavy jag.

"Nice songs, Sal," slurred McCatty. "Let me . . ."

Without warning, Sal produced a two-shot derringer from the folds of the petticoats beneath her long dress. She stuck the barrel into one of McCatty's nostrils and cocked the hammer.

"I'm glad you liked the tunes, mister," said Sal in a low growl that resembled that of a cat preparing to pounce on another feline, "but if you don't get your hands off my downside, I'll make certain you never smell another flower the rest of your life."

McCatty's eyes crossed as they concentrated on the gun in Sal's hand, and his hands shot out to each side of him as he complied with her demand. Sal released the hammer of the pistol slowly and replaced it inside the garter-belt holster on her thigh.

"That's better, sugar," cooed Sal with a friendlier smile.

"I didn't mean any harm," pleaded McCatty.

"I know that," sympathized Sal. She bent quickly and pecked the miner on the end of his nose with a kiss. "Now that we know where we stand maybe you'll buy me a drink later. How about that?"

"Sure thing, Sal."

"Good, but like I said, later. Right now I've got to visit with an old friend."

Sal gave McCatty a wink and continued on to Mordecai's table. Another man reached out for her as she passed, but she anticipated the grasp and slapped it away. At last, she made it to her destination.

"Well, if it isn't Beecher Hay," said Sal, interrupting the conversation at the table. "How are you, you old skinflint?"

"Just fine, Sal," answered Hay with a devilish grin. "How about you?"

"Still clicking nickels," she replied.

"Odd that you should say that, Sal." Hay laughed. "This gentleman's name just happens to be Nichols."

"Is that right?" She gave the big prospector a quick once-over. "How do you do, Mr. Nichols?"

Remembering his manners, Nichols rose to greet the lady. "I'm pleased to make your acquaintance, Miss Macomb."

Sal's eyes followed the miner's face as he stood. "Well, you can call me Sal."

"I'd rather call you Sarah," said Nichols, his eyes locked on hers.

"How did you know my real name?" quizzed Sal.

"I told him what it was," joined in Mordecai. The journalist jumped to his feet. "Mordecai Courtney, publisher and editor of the Carthage City *Clarion*, at your service, Miss Macomb."

"Oh, I get it," said Sal with a coy smile aimed at Nichols, nearly ignoring Mordecai. "You've a ventriloquist act, right, Mr. Nichols? And this is your dummy? You're good. Maybe I can use you sometime."

The humor rolled over Mordecai, but he didn't care because no one was really laughing at him. He was too excited by the fact that Louisiana Sal had taken an interest in his friend.

"Very clever, Miss Macomb," Mordecai smiled. "Won't you join us?"

"Thanks, I will."

Mordecai surrendered his chair to Sal, and after she was seated, Nichols sat down again.

Harry Willit cleared his throat for attention.

"Forgive me, Sal," said Hay. "This gentleman is Mr. Harry Willit. He owns the local dry-goods store."

With the introductions completed, another round of drinks was brought to the table by George Bemis. Mordecai was imbibing, but Nichols remained true to his conviction that alcohol was evil personified.

"Getting acquainted, Sal?" asked Bemis.

"Trying to," said Sal.

Hay paid for the refreshments, and Bemis went back to the bar.

"Well, Beecher, what brings you way up here?" inquired Sal. "Come to steal the mines?"

Hay was unflushed and with good humor replied, "Why, Sal, what makes you say such nonsense? You know me better than that." The last contained a caution that she should steer away from mentioning the past.

"Yeah, right, I do. You're as honest as they come." She turned away from the mining executive. "Well, Mr. Nichols, what do you do for a living? Wrestle grizzly bears with your hands tied behind your back? It's easy enough to see that you certainly have the build for it."

With that, the talk became light banter, and Beecher Hay's true purpose for being in Carthage City remained confidential, although the secret now was shared by three.

When Sal left them to round up her girls for another set of songs, Mordecai also excused himself, saying that he had to finish the next number of the *Clarion*. As he walked back to the newspaper, the journalist was a little tipsy, and he rather relished the feeling. Recounting the events and words of the evening, he was suddenly overtaken with an uncontrollable urge to continue the celebration of the Golden Palace's opening, even if he had to do it on his own. He drew the Remington from its hiding place inside the waistband of his trousers and fired it into the air, not once, but four times, and after each shot, he gave forth a high-pitched hurrah. The reverberations from the gun, which were barely louder than the crack of a teamster's snake, went unnoticed by the other celebrants of the town.

As soon as Sal sang the final note of the third song, Russ Nichols left the Golden Palace and made straight for Mordecai's building. He saw a light glowing inside and realized that Mordecai was still working. He tried the door and found it unlocked. He entered the office quietly and approached Mordecai, who had his back to him. The journalist was busy setting type. A board creaked beneath the miner's boots.

Much to Nichols' surprise, Mordecai spun around to face him. The click of the Remington's hammer falling on an empty cartridge stunned the prospector's ears. He blinked several times before actually seeing the pistol in Mordecai's hand.

"Russ, it's you!"

"Good God, Mordecai!" blurted Nichols,

regaining his senses. "You could have killed me!"

Mordecai stared down at the revolver, the revelation of what possibly could have happened shocking him into instant sobriety.

"Where did you get that thing?" demanded Nichols, still slightly unnerved but also angered.

"I bought it from Harry Willit," said Mordecai meekly, as if to blame the incident on the storekeeper. His eyes were still fixed on the gun, which he continued to aim at Nichols.

"For God's sake, put it away before you do kill me."

"Oh, yes," mumbled Mordecai as he started to put the weapon back into his pants.

"No," said Nichols, "put it away in a drawer or something. You shouldn't be carrying that thing around. It can only cause you trouble. Just think what might have happened if you'd had that thing when Mallory was giving you Old Ned the other day."

"He wouldn't have slapped me the way he did," challenged Mordecai.

"That's right, he wouldn't. He would have shot you instead, and now you'd be buried alongside those three cowboys he did kill."

"Maybe."

"No maybes about it, Mordecai. You'd be

132

dead, and that's all there is to it. Men like Mallory didn't gain their reputations by being slow to act. If you'd drawn a gun on him, he would have sent you to the next world straightaway. He knows how to handle a gun. You don't."

"I don't know about that." Mordecai grinned. "I got the drop on you pretty quick."

"Okay, I'll grant you that much, but supposing I had been someone out to do you wrong and I had been heeled. Then what? You'd be dead on the floor, that's what. Now put that thing away, and don't ever carry it again. It will only bring you trouble."

"I suppose you're right." Mordecai opened a drawer and put the Remington inside it. He slid the tray back into place. "I rather enjoyed carrying it."

"Why?" asked Nichols as he sat down in the extra chair.

Mordecai shrugged. "I don't know for certain. I guess it made me feel that I was the same size as everyone else. Yeah, I guess that's it."

"My friend," said Nichols with a soft, paternal tone in his voice, "you don't need a gun to be another man's equal. You already have a great equalizer in this newspaper. Just owning and publishing it makes you the equal of every man in town; maybe even the superior to most. Mordecai, your talent with words is greater than all the guns in Carthage City. No man can stand up to you when it comes to that."

The journalist contemplated the miner. "Do you really believe that, Russ?"

"I wouldn't have said it if I didn't."

"You know, I've always been small, and bigger people have pushed me around for as long as I can remember. I think that's why I chose this profession. It's the only way I can strike back."

"That's right, it is," agreed Nichols, "but you shouldn't look at this newspaper as a tool for vengeance. Think of all the good it can do. That's how you should use it. This newspaper can make things happen, and you're the man who's making this newspaper speak. This newspaper is really you talking. It talks and people listen. That makes you a bigger man than most because you have the ears of your fellows. Is that not so?"

"You know, I never thought of it like that." Mordecai's face brightened with a happy smile. "Yes, you're right, Russ. I am bigger than most."

"Now don't go overboard with that kind of thinking," cautioned Nichols. "You're still a half-pint runt. You get to talking too big, like

134

you did with Mallory, and someone with less conscience is going to put a hole in you with a piece of hot lead."

Unoffended by the former remark, Mordecai acknowledged the wisdom in Nichols' statement. "I see what you mean. I'll try to keep my enthusiasm under control."

"Okay," said Nichols. "Now that we've settled that point, let's move on to the reason why I came here tonight."

"Yes, why did you sneak in here like you did?"

"I wasn't sneaking," denied Nichols. "I just happen to be very quiet when I walk. That's besides the point anyway. I came here to talk to you about this Hay fellow."

"You might as well know the truth," said Mordecai, coming straight out with it. "He really isn't a banker."

"I thought as much," said Nichols, "although he does reek of money."

"He's vice president of Southwest Arizona Mining Company," explained Mordecai.

"Never heard of them. Why did he say he was a banker?"

"It was only a mild lie," stuttered Mordecai.

"And you went along with it. Why?"

Mordecai related the interview he had had that afternoon with Hay, and Nichols listened attentively.

"I see," said the miner. "It was your idea, but he agreed to it."

"Yes, he did."

"Well, something strikes me curious about this Hay. It was the way Miss Macomb greeted him. They acted as if they were old friends, but they didn't say anything about it. I'm wondering why they behaved in such a manner."

"Now that you mention it," said Mordecai, "I'm also finding that to be a curiosity. Why do you suppose they played down the relationship."

"From the way Hay reacted to her question about stealing the mines, I should think he has something to hide, and that means he's a man not to be trusted."

"Oh, I wouldn't go that far, Russ. Besides, I saw nothing in his reaction that would indicate such an assumption."

"Maybe not," reconsidered Nichols, "but I still think we should keep an eye on him. It was just something in the way Miss Macomb greeted him, and it has me worried."

"Don't lose any sleep over it, Russ. I'm sure everything will work out for the better. Just wait and see."

Nichols stood up. "You say Hay wants to meet with all the miners? Well, you might take him on a tour of the mines tomorrow. That way he can meet every one of us individually, and then we can hold a meeting once he makes up his mind what he's going to do."

"A capital idea, Russ. I'll bring him up to your diggings first thing in the morning, as soon as I get the newspaper out."

"I'll see you then," said Nichols as he departed.

Mordecai waved a farewell, then sat back to consider the conversation which had just concluded. As he mulled over the miner's concerns, he decided that it would be wise for him to have a talk with Louisiana Sal Macomb and find out what she knew about Hay. He wrote himself a note to remind him to do just that at the earliest possible opportunity.

CHAPTER 9

Beecher Hay had been on a business trip to New York when he learned of the new discoveries in the Burro Mountains. He was riding the Southern Pacific's Lone Star Express when a yellowed copy of the Carthage City *Clarion* fell out of a box of trash the porter was carrying through the car. As the black bent over to retrieve the tabloid, Hay saw the ten-point headline about Deke McCatty's find.

"Let me see that, boy," ordered Hay.

"Yes, sir," drawled the porter. He handed the paper to the mining executive, then went on his way.

Hay read the article with great interest. In fact, he read the entire edition, including the advertisements. They were all very informative, telling him that Carthage City was a growing and prosperous town but that it didn't have any large mining company operating there as yet. He reflected on that aspect for less than a minute before deciding to telegraph Southwest's chairman of the board of directors in New York.

The train laid over in Houston for an hour, time enough for Hay to send the wire. He said in it that he thought Carthage City was worth investigating as soon as possible, and he requested that, if the chairman's response was positive, an engineer be sent to Carthage City to meet him. He would continue on to Baton Rouge, and the reply should be sent there.

As soon as the locomotive halted in the Louisiana capital, Hay hurried to the telegrapher's office and asked if there was a telegram for him. There was. The head of Southwest's corporate structure agreed with him that he should return to New Mexico immediately and size up the prospects of locating a stamp mill in Carthage City. He also stated that engineer Sven Ulven was being sent to meet him in Carthage City. "And by the way," the message read, "where in the blazes is Carthage City?"

Hay laughed out loud at the last, then realized that he wasn't sure where in the blazes Carthage City was. He answered his superior's question by stating that it was somewhere near the border and west of El Paso, knowing fully that the elderly gentleman wouldn't know one town from the next even if he had a map in front of him.

Along the railroad line Hay inquired as to the locality of Carthage City, and much to his chagrin, no one seemed to have heard of the new community. Not until he reached Lordsburg did Hay finally discover the exact location of Carthage City. That made him very happy, but when he learned that the only way to reach the mountain village was to hire a buckboard or buy a horse, he wasn't pleased at all. He had hoped that a stagecoach line had been enterprising enough to establish a route to Carthage City, but none had. With that out of the question, he opted for the saddle as the least expensive of conveyances.

Until Mordecai mentioned Sarah Macomb, Hay's plans were proceeding exactly as he had made them while riding up from Lordsburg, but the presence of an old acquaintance, someone who knew him too well, caused him to reconsider certain portions of the strategy. He would have to talk softly in Carthage City as long as Louisiana Sal was there.

Hay had good reason to fear the dance-hall singer. After all, she had been the one person in La Paz to see through his scheme to gain control of the mines in that Arizona boomtown. Sal had recognized Hay as a swindler, albeit a scoundrel who used the law and other men's ignorance of it to his distinct advantage, and when he attempted to apply pressure on the miners to sell their claims for ridiculously small amounts of cash, Sal organized the men into resisting Hay. Sal hadn't counted on Hay owning the local sheriff. With Hay's insistence, the lawman ordered Sal to take herself and her girls elsewhere. Once she was out of the way, Hay had little difficulty in persuading the prospectors to accept his offers. Of course, the deaths of two of their leaders in mining "accidents" might have helped him, too.

For her part, Sal knew Beecher Hay for the man he was. As for business, he would stop at nothing to attain what he wanted, but apart from his occupation, Hay was as congenial as any that came along her way. He was humorous with his conversation, and he was free with his money when he was in a saloon. If it wasn't for his heartless business acumen, Sal would have liked the man, but she didn't. As she sat with Hay, Willit, and Nichols in the Bonanza Room, she wondered if Hay was planning to acquire the mines around Carthage City in the same manner which he had employed in La Paz. After the last show that night, Sal learned the answer to that question when Hay met her in the hall outside her room.

"Well, Beecher, I thought you'd be coming around." Sal stood with her back to the door to her lodging.

"Now, Sal, there's no reason to take that tone with me. We're old friends."

"No, we aren't, Beecher, and you know it."

"You're still holding a grudge, aren't you, Sal? You shouldn't, you know. If you'd kept that pretty nose out of my business, I could have gotten you bookings in San Francisco."

"I don't need your help to get to San Francisco."

Hay's face contorted with anger. "Look here, Sal. I won't tolerate you interfering here like you did in La Paz. If you get in my way again, I won't be as easy on you this time. Is that clear?"

"Don't get yourself all lathered up, Beecher. I'm not going to stick my neck out again for a bunch of men who don't know when to come in out of the cold. If this bunch here is as stupid as those in La Paz, then you're welcome to them. Go ahead and take them for all their worth, but be sure you leave them drinking money. My girls and I have to make a living, too."

Hay smiled. "That's the right attitude, Sal. You're a smart girl. You're making the right move here, and I'll see to it that you're properly rewarded."

"Go to hell, Beecher. I don't want your gratitude or your money. You keep your distance, and I'll keep mine. Is that good enough for you?"

"Okay, we'll play it your way. Good night, Sal."

The next morning when Hay awakened in his hotel-room bed he wondered if Sal would keep her promise of the night before. Just in case she had second thoughts, he made up his mind to acquire a little insurance.

Mordecai was up with the sun. He ate a breakfast of eggs and side pork, then went to work printing the latest number of the *Clarion*. It took him an hour to crank out the front page and another hour to press the back. By eight o'clock, he was ready to meet Beecher Hay at the Golden Palace.

George Bemis was just taking his place behind the bar when Mordecai entered the Bonanza Room. It was obvious by the bags under his eyes that he had slept little. His morning man handed him a cup of black coffee, and Mordecai presented the saloonkeeper with a newspaper.

"Good morning, George." Mordecai smiled.

"How can you be so cheery at this hour of the day, Mordecai?" moaned Bemis.

"This is a banner day for Carthage City, George. We should all be happy."

Bemis sipped the java and scanned the front page of the *Clarion*. The headline announcing Hay's arrival and true business in the mountain town drew his close scrutiny.

"I thought this Hay fellow was a banker," said Bemis.

"I am actually," said Hay as he entered the barroom. "I own the bank in La Paz, Arizona."

"But it says here that you're a vice president for a mining outfit."

"That's also true." Hay smiled. "Among my other business interests is a steamboat line which hauls freight and passengers up and down the Colorado River. I'm president of the Arizona Riverboat Company. You see, Mr. Bemis, I am a man with many hats."

"Yes, I can see that."

"Good morning, Mr. Hay," greeted Mordecai. "I trust you slept well."

"Indeed, I did, Mr. Courtney. The accommodations in this fine establishment are quite *le beau*, don't you agree?"

Not knowing what the French phrase meant, Mordecai could only agree with Hay. "Most assuredly, Mr. Hay. They are definitely *lay-bow*."

Hay smiled with the knowledge that he had

the better of the journalist, but he was above explaining the term and thus embarrassing Mordecai. Hay shifted his attention to the newspapers in Mordecai's hand.

"May I purchase a copy?"

"Forget the charge," said Mordecai as he handed a sheet to Hay. "Enjoy it as part of our continued good relations." He hesitated before continuing. "I sense that you have yet to eat, Mr. Hay."

"No, I have just now come down from my room."

"In that case, will you excuse me? I have some deliveries to make."

"Certainly, Mr. Courtney."

"I shouldn't be more than an hour. As soon as I'm finished, I would like to take you on a tour of the mines, and, at the same time, introduce you to those men who have been fortunate thus far."

"Very good, Mr. Courtney. I'll have my morning meal and wait for your return."

True to his word, Mordecai was back at the Golden Palace within the hour. He and Hay walked down the street to Jack Eldon's livery stable and blacksmith shop. Eldon's teen-age son, Dan, saddled their mounts, and they were off for Russ Nichols' claim, reaching it within fifteen minutes. They dismounted at the mine entrance, and Mordecai stuck his head inside the shaft to call for the miner.

"Be out in a minute, Mordecai," echoed Nichols' reply.

While they waited, Hay scanned the area, noting the amount of rock piled nearby. It was easy to see the gold in the quartz. Already he knew the value of the Lucky Nickel Mine.

"Morning, Mordecai," said Nichols as he stepped into the daylight. "Mr. Hay." He nodded at the mining executive.

"How are you this fine day, Mr. Nichols?" beamed Hay.

"Passable," grunted Nichols.

"Glad to hear it."

There was a definite silence between the men, almost as if each was waiting for the others to continue the small talk. At last, Hay resumed the conversation.

"Well, Mr. Nichols, our mutual friend here tells me that he has already confided in you about who I really am and why I am here."

"That's right, he did."

"Well, then, would you mind if I looked inside your tunnel?"

"A tunnel has two openings, Mr. Hay. A mine shaft has only one."

Hay was taken aback by the lesson in English. "Uh, yes, of course."

"All the same," continued Nichols, "help yourself. There's a lantern inside. It should keep you from stumbling over any loose rocks."

"Thank you." Hay smiled before disappearing into the mountain hole.

"You didn't have to be rude," scolded Mordecai.

Nichols snake-eyed his diminutive friend. "What I said last night still goes."

"Now, Russ," groaned Mordecai, "this is neither the time nor the place to discuss the matter of the gentleman's integrity."

"Mordecai, if you could bottle that malarkey, all the farmers in the country would beat a path to your door to buy it. Trouble is, I'm not a plow jockey, so I don't have any use for it. Do you get my meaning?"

"I still say . . ."

"Do you get my meaning?" repeated Nichols, a decibel louder.

Mordecai sighed. "You've made your position quite clear, Russ."

The sound of Hay's footsteps ended their talk.

"I must say, Mr. Nichols," said Hay upon rejoining them, "that you've done a remarkable amount of excavating here — remarkable for one man, that is. I hope it's all been profitable."

"So far, it's been decent. The future depends, of course."

Hay smiled warmly. "Yes, of course. Well, I've seen enough here, Mr. Courtney. I hope you'll attend the meeting this evening, Mr. Nichols."

"I guess every man in town will be there wanting to hear what you've got to offer, Mr. Hay."

"I certainly hope so. Good day, Mr. Nichols."

Mordecai spent the better part of the next four hours leading Hay around the slopes of the canyon. Hay was as amiable with those men who had yet to strike pay dirt as he was with those who had. He encouraged all of them to continue their works, saying they could never know when the next shovel of soil or the next chunk of quartz would turn out to be filled with gold. By the time they had finished the round, Mordecai was certain that he had Hay's speech memorized.

"I am apt to believe, Mr. Hay," said Mordecai as they rode for town, "that you may have missed your calling."

"How is that, sir?"

"From the palaver you have just this day delivered to the prospectors, I should think you would be a great success in politics."

Hay broke into such uncontrollable laughter that he was near to falling from the saddle before Mordecai reached over to assist him.

"You are so correct, Mr. Courtney," said Hay after regaining his composure. "More so than you think. You see, I was once in the political game. I served a portion of New York as a congressman, but that was during the war. My three terms ran from '62 to '68. Then President Grant appointed me to a post in the War Department. After a tour of the military forts out here in the West, I decided to return to business. Thus my current position."

"It sounds as if you've had a most interesting life," remarked Mordecai.

"I have little room for complaint. Besides, there is no time allowed for the complainer in life. Don't you find this to be true?"

"Most assuredly."

Once they were back at the Golden Palace, Hay was promptly greeted by a tall young man who appeared to be of Nordic extraction. It was Sven Ulven, the engineer sent by the chairman of the board of directors of Southwest Arizona Mining. Hay greeted the bespectacled Swede warmly and introduced him to Mordecai. After learning that Ulven had already eaten lunch, Hay instructed him to begin his work immediately.

"I want you to ride around this area and determine where we could best locate our mill. You might also drop in on some of the miners and inspect their properties. I've already done this, but since you talk their language, your expert eye will be appreciated. Not being an engineer, I could very well have missed something that could prove valuable to us at a later date. Report back to me as soon as you're finished. I'll be here waiting for you, Ulven."

The graduate of Minnesota College of Mines nodded and departed.

"A quiet lad," remarked Hay to Mordecai, "but very capable in his field. He was born in Sweden and came over with his family before the war."

"A hardy folk, those Swedes," said Mordecai in passing.

"Yes," agreed Hay. "They'll make good Americans one day." He noticed that his coat was dusty and brushed at a sleeve. "It seems that I've brought some of the road back with me. I think I should retire to my room and refresh myself before dining. If you'll excuse me, Mr. Courtney?"

"Certainly, sir. I was thinking that I should do the same."

Hay exited through the doorway to the hotel lobby, and Mordecai made for the street entrance to the Bonanza Room. As he reached the swinging doors, he heard his name called. He turned to see Louisiana Sal approaching him.

"Mr. Courtney, how are you this day?" she asked.

"Quite fine, Miss Macomb, and you?"

"Still clicking nickels," said Sal with a friendly smile. She took Mordecai by an arm. "I was wondering if you wouldn't buy me a drink."

Mordecai was surprised by the invitation. Of course, he had wanted to interview her, so he thought this would be as good a time as any, although he was planning to leave the premises.

"Well, I was . . ."

"Please, Mr. Courtney," said Sal in a hurried, hushed voice, another surprise to Mordecai, "I need to talk to you."

Mordecai was confounded by her urgency. As much as he had wanted to confer with Sal, he found this switch to be a curious turn of events. Although hesitant, he decided to accept.

"Why, certainly, I'll buy you a drink. It would be both an honor and a pleasure to sip with you."

"Thank you, Mr. Courtney," sighed Sal. She scanned the hall for the right table for them.

Pinky John Mallory had a game going with a couple of drifters in the front, but the rest of the room was vacant. More like the dance-hall hustler that she was, Sal added, "Let's sit in the back, Mr. Courtney, where we can be alone."

"Certainly, my dear," said Mordecai as he gazed up at her eyes.

"White wine for me, Georgie," said Sal as she led the journalist past the bar.

"I believe I'll have the same," ordered Mordecai.

Bemis had their drinks for them almost as soon as they sat down at the table. Mordecai fished four bits out of his trouser pocket and paid for the refreshments, and Bemis left them alone.

"Now, Miss Macomb, what seems to be so important this fine day?"

"You've got trouble coming your way, Mr. Courtney."

"Trouble?"

"Beecher Hay is a crook."

"Mr. Hay?"

"Will you quit interrupting me? I'm trying to save your hide, so will you shut up and listen?"

"Proceed, Miss Macomb."

Sal went on to tell Mordecai everything she knew about Beecher Hay and his method of operation, which wasn't everything there was to know about the man. For instance, Sal didn't know about what had happened in La Paz after she was run out of town. But she did know that Hay was caught grafting while he was in the War Department and that the scandal had been hushed up.

"This news astounds me, Miss Macomb," said Mordecai, almost as if he wasn't believing the lady.

"It's all true, Mr. Courtney."

"If it is," mumbled Mordecai, "then Russ was right about him."

"Who?"

"Uh, Mr. Nichols," explained Mordecai. "He told me last night that he held reservations as to the integrity of Mr. Hay."

Sal smiled. "He's right. Hay can't be trusted." She looked up to see the mining executive entering the barroom at that moment from the hotel lobby. "There he is now. We'd better break this up." Then louder, she added, "Well, thanks for the drink, Mr. Courtney. It was nice. I hope you've got all the information you need for that article."

"Yes, indeed, I have, Miss Macomb," said Mordecai, maintaining the charade. "Thank you for your cooperation."

"Anytime."

Sal stood and walked for the stairs which led

up to the rooms above. She was careful not to look in Hay's direction. The temptation for her to turn at the top of the steps in order to see if Hay was watching her was great, but she resisted the urge.

Mordecai pushed himself away from the table and stepped over to the bar where Hay was partaking of a free lunch and a cold beer.

"Mind if I join you, Mr. Hay?"

"Not at all. It would please me to have your company."

As the two men spent the afternoon exchanging stories about their pasts, Mordecai grew confident that the interview with Louisiana Sal had gone unnoticed by Hay, and even if he had observed them together, it was only at the last minute after Sal had seen Hay enter the room. Whichever, Mordecai was positive that they had deceived Hay.

As dusk approached, the miners began drifting into the saloon for the meeting Hay had requested them to attend. Also, Sven Ulven returned from his inspection of the vicinity. He immediately conferred with Hay in private, then sat down for a glass of lager and a thick beefsteak.

When Russ Nichols came into the Golden Palace alone, Mordecai hurried over to him. Knowing that most of the men followed

Nichols' lead, Mordecai thought to tell him of the knowledge concerning Hay that he had learned from Sal and then convince Nichols to organize the prospectors against Hay. But the journalist didn't get a chance to speak more than a greeting.

"Gentlemen," said Hay in a loud voice from the stage at the rear of the barroom, "if I can have your attention, we can start this meeting and finish our business in plenty of time before the ladies are due to perform. Please be seated and we'll begin."

The crowd settled into all the available chairs, and those who remained standing did so at the bar or against the wall. Everyone ceased their chatter.

"First off," said Hay, "allow me to congratulate you on this fine community which you've begun in these mountains. I'm certain future generations will always remember the sweat and toil each and every one gave to this town."

"Remember what I said about malarkey?" Nichols asked Mordecai. "He's in the same business as you are."

"Russ, I must talk to you," said Mordecai.

"After the meeting, Mordecai."

"But, Russ, I . . . umph . . ."

Nichols muffled Mordecai's mouth with a big hand.

"After the meeting, Mordecai."

"Now to business," continued Hay. "I am pleased to announce that my engineer, Mr. Sven Ulven, has confirmed what I suspected this afternoon when I was visiting your claims with Mr. Courtney, and that is that there is sufficient gold in these mountains to warrant Southwest Arizona Mining Company building a stamp mill in Carthage City." A loud hurrah went up from everyone but Mordecai and Nichols. "Thank you, gentlemen, but as I was saying, that is the good news."

"Here it comes," whispered Nichols.

"The bad news is the cost of constructing such a mill will be very high, and thus Southwest will not be able to purchase your claims for what you might consider their full worth to be. For you twenty-three men who have already found gold, Southwest is offering $5,000 for your claims, and for you men who haven't been so fortunate, we are offering $500 and a job once operations are in full swing."

Just as Hay expected, there was a buzz of talk, both pro and con, among the audience. He waited patiently for the men to quiet down.

"Mr. Hay!" called Russ Nichols from the front of the barroom. His voice stemmed the rumble between him and the mining executive.

"Yes, Mr. Nichols?" beamed Hay, confident that Nichols was about to accept the proposal.

"Mr. Hay, I'm not speaking for anyone but myself," began Nichols, "but I would like to say something about your offer for my claim."

Hay's smile grew wider with expectation. All he needed was for a man like Nichols to go along with him and all of Carthage City would follow. This town was going to be easier than La Paz.

"Please go right ahead, Mr. Nichols."

Every man in the joint turned to listen to Nichols.

"Russ, I . . ."

Nichols again clamped his hand over Mordecai's mouth.

"Not now, Mordecai," Nichols whispered out of the side of his mouth. Then to Hay and all the others, he said, "Like I mentioned before, I'm only speaking for me. That offer you just made, Mr. Hay?"

The room was totally silent.

"Yes, Mr. Nichols?"

"It stinks to hell!"

CHAPTER 10

All the words that Mordecai printed in the next number of the *Clarion* in support of the miners' position against Hay didn't express their feelings as succinctly as Russ Nichols had with his four-syllable statement. Hay had tried to placate the prospectors with more flowery phrases, but the men were having none of it as they shouted him down from the stage. Angered by their attitude, Hay stormed out of the meeting, and the next morning he was in Mordecai's office seeking the journalist's aid in settling the matter.

"Mr. Courtney, I come to you because it's obvious that you are the only man in this town with the power to reason coherently. I am a businessman who thinks in dollars and cents, and I feel I have made a fair and just offer to the miners for their properties. I think you can agree with that."

He waited for Mordecai to confirm his assumption, but the newspaperman remained silent on the subject.

"Well, as I was saying," continued Hay, "I think the offer was equitable, but I will withdraw it completely if the miners don't come to their collective senses very soon. In the meantime, I will inform my superiors that the construction of a stamp mill in this vicinity would be a profitable venture for Southwest to undertake. Since there is no telegraph as yet in this town, I am riding to Lordsburg today to wire New York. If anyone should have a change of heart, I may be reached there.

"In the meantime, Mr. Courtney, I implore you to use your powers as a journalist and as a leading citizen of this community to persuade the miners to see the folly of their stand. I cannot and will not increase the figures already mentioned. That is my only offer, and I wish you would influence the men to see the justice of it. Will you do so, Mr. Courtney, for the benefit of all concerned?"

Mordecai cast an appreciative eye on the mining executive, thinking that Hay had almost convinced him to act as the gentleman desired. In his younger years, Mordecai would have been easily swayed by such a man of wealth, but past experience had taught him the opposite. As he studied his visitor briefly, the man Mordecai had become calculated a response.

"Mr. Hay, I shall endeavor to fulfill your request to act for the benefit of all concerned. It is not only my obligation to do so but my highest goal. The future of Carthage City lies within my province to help or hinder as I so please. Rest assured, sir, that I will respond according to the former, and all shall rise to the pinnacle of success for it."

Hay was dumb-struck. In the confusion of his mind, he couldn't decide whether Mordecai had said yes or no to his question. He was hopeful that the journalist had been affirmative.

"Well put, sir," congratulated Hay. He stood and proffered his hand in farewell.

"Thank you, sir," said Mordecai, accepting the handshake reluctantly, "and a safe journey to Lordsburg."

The issue in which Mordecai supported the miners' stand against Hay reached Lordsburg within the week, and a copy was immediately purchased by the mining executive. To say the least, he was enraged. With a *Clarion* in one hand and the other flailing at the air, he paced his hotel room in a tirade that only Sven Ulven was present to hear.

"The little viper lied to me!" shouted Hay. "I should have known not to trust him. Now he has them stirred up against me, and I'll never get those mines for a profit."

"Does this mean we won't be building the mill?" asked Ulven.

"Of course, it doesn't!" snapped Hay. "That part of our plans will go ahead as scheduled. In the meantime, we have other fish to catch and fry."

Ulven had no idea what Hay had in mind, but the vice president of the Southwest Arizona Mining knew exactly what his next step would be.

Hay's first call of the day was on Bert Wooley, the publisher of the Lordsburg *Leader*. Knowing how active the competition was between the *Clarion* and Wooley's publication, Hay thought to stir up trouble for Mordecai and the people of Carthage City.

"I tell you, Mr. Wooley," Hay was saying, "Carthage City is nothing but a new version of Sodom and Gomorrah. Sin abounds everywhere within the town. Lewd women parade themselves for the men. If a man has one drink too many, he awakens the next morning with an empty pocket to accompany his swollen head. Not a night passes that someone isn't shot to death in the street or in one of the

161

several filthy saloons. They have a gambler up there named Mallory . . ."

"Pinky John Mallory?" inquired Wooley.

"You've heard of him, I see." Hay smirked. "Yes, the same man. He killed three poor cowboys who caught him cheating at cards, and to make matters worse, the town condoned the murders. The man is still there, a threat to anyone who has the grit to call his play."

Wooley was a stocky man of middle age, going bald rapidly and suffering from an ulcer brought on by too much alcohol and worry over his future. His face was unshaven and had been so for the better part of a week, which only served to accent the soiled cuffs of his gray shirt. With stubby fingers working voraciously at holding a nubbin of a pencil, he scribbled notes of everything Hay reported.

"And what's more, Mr. Wooley, the town harbors criminals of the nth degree. Why, in my short stay, I overheard more than one conversation between the roughest-appearing characters who were either boasting about one escapade or were planning another. I believe that one of the men was the notorious William Bonney."

"Billy the Kid is in Carthage City?" queried Wooley. "This is news that Pat Garrett will be happy to learn."

"Oh, there's more, Mr. Wooley. Just as I was leaving the town, I was passed by a group of men on horseback, and by the looks of their leader, I would swear he was none other than Curly Bill Brocius."

"Curly Bill, too?"

"Yes, indeed, sir. Cathrage City is nothing more than a den of vipers, unsafe for decent men and women. Why, sir, I would not advise any man who values his possessions, not to speak of his life, to visit Carthage City. I thank the great Almighty that I am here today to repeat my adventure to you."

Wherever Hay had failed to exaggerate, Wooley added his own personal touch of magnification to the mining executive's version of life in Carthage City. The number of the Lordsburg *Leader* which spread the tale was in such demand throughout the entire territory that Wooley had to print extra copies.

Hay wasn't finished. Every hardcase he came across, including some old acquaintances from La Paz, he hired to travel to Carthage City for a short visit, telling them that the town was free of lawmen and that the pickings were ripe for a man with a quick hand.

Before the ink was dry on the *Leader*'s next edition, the dregs of the Southwest began arriving in Carthage City. Mordecai noted their coming. George Bemis had told him that this was to be expected in a boomtown, so Mordecai was rather nonchalant over the entire matter until a copy of the *Leader* was presented to him.

"George, have you seen this?" asked Mordecai as he entered the Bonanza Room that afternoon. He waved the *Leader* ahead of him as he scampered up to the bar.

"What's that, Mordecai?" asked Bemis.

"This tripe in the Lordsburg paper, that's what." He spread the newspaper on the counter for Bemis to peruse. "Just look at that pack of lies! Nothing but lies, I tell you, and all about Carthage City being a town of iniquity. Can you imagine the gall of the man who printed that? I swear, he should be horse-whipped and the sooner the better. Tar and feathers would be too good for him."

Bemis was listening to Mordecai with only one ear. He was too occupied with the farce he was reading to pay any great attention to the journalist.

"Did you hear me, George?"

"What was that, Mordecai?"

"I was saying that we ought to ride down to Lordsburg and drag this fellow Wooley from his hole and give the rat a free ride on a rail."

"I don't believe a measure that drastic is

called for, Mordecai."

"Then what do you suggest we do about this?"

"You're a newspaperman, Mordecai. You should know how to combat something like this. If you don't, maybe you should look for another trade."

"That won't be necessary, my friend. You're right, I do know how to handle Mr. Wooley."

"I'll tell you one thing, Mordecai. This explains why our population has suddenly swelled. It's almost as if someone wanted it to be that way. You know, someone who wants this to come true so he can gain from it."

"Someone like Beecher Hay?"

"You named him, I didn't."

"Well, we'll see about this."

Mordecai hardly had the chance to pen one word of retaliation before Carthage City became exactly what Wooley described in the *Leader*. The town became divided into two factions: the miners and the cowboys. A third group, a very small minority, remained neutral. These were the businessmen and a few odd fellows like Pinky John Mallory. They kept to themselves mostly, waiting to see which side would gain the advantage.

The vigilance committee, with Russ Nichols at its head, proved to be a futile gesture at law and order. None of the men, including Nichols, wanted a confrontation with the cowboys. It was argued that they wouldn't stand to win a gunfight with the toughs, even though the opposition was disorganized and had no leader.

The situation finally came to a head one night at the Golden Palace. A young cowboy ordered a drink at the bar, and when Bemis demanded to see the color of his money first, the wrangler drew his six-shooter and pointed it at the barkeeper's face.

"This is all I need to get a drink around here," said the cowboy. "Now pour or eat lead."

"Leave that bottle where it is, barkeep," said a man near the door.

Bemis looked past the gunman to see a mustachioed stranger in a black suit and white shirt with a black string tie standing just inside the swinging doors. The saloonkeeper didn't know who the stranger was who had a Winchester trained on the youth.

The drifter saw the stranger's image in the mirror over the backbar. "I said to pour," he snarled, ignoring the stranger's commanding position.

"If I was you, son, I'd put that shooting iron away while I was still able to do it." The stranger cocked the rifle. "You see, this piece of mine only asks once, then it goes to shooting."

Suddenly there was a loud commotion as the rest of the saloon's customers found cover. Realizing that he was at a disadvantage, the cowpoke decided to back down. He raised his revolver slowly over his head and turned to face his challenger.

"Okay, mister, you got the drop on me. I'm calling it quits." He started to put the six-gun back in its holster.

"Not good enough, son. Just let it drop to the floor and kick it over here."

"You ain't taking my gun."

With that, the cowboy tried to drop to one knee to take aim, but a flash and a roar from the Winchester interrupted the movement. The .45-caliber slug ripped through his chest just above the heart.

The rifle held its aim on the victim as the stranger walked across the room toward the corpse. With a quick turn of his boot, he flipped the dead man over onto his back.

"Young hotheads never learn, do they?" He spat into the nearest cuspidor. "Did you know him?"

"Just a drifter," said Bemis, who had been the only witness to the shooting.

The rifleman turned to the crowd, which was just then coming out of hiding. "Okay, some of you boys get him out of here. Take him out to wherever it is you bury trash like this, and put him in the ground. You can divvy up whatever he has that's of any value."

No one moved.

"Boys, my name is Pete Spencer. I'm the new marshal of this town."

Four men stepped forward immediately and carried out the marshal's orders.

Pete Spencer's arrival in Carthage City was a moment for every law-abiding citizen to celebrate, according to the *Clarion*. The lawless, on the other hand, pondered their fates, and several drifted out of town in the same manner as they had come.

Beecher Hay's return to Carthage City was noted in the same issue of the *Clarion*, but the fanfare was missing from the article, which was relegated to the back page. Instead, Mordecai saw fit to include Hay in his editorial about the men who abused the law. Hay merely ignored the commentary, deciding that there were other ways to deal with Mordecai and the miners.

Within the week, Carthage City was clear of most of its troublemakers. The marshal's reputation, an exaggerated notability promulgated by Mordecai in the pages of his tabloid, was highly responsible for the accomplishment. The journalist recounted the facts of Spencer's career in law enforcing, and after considering them, he increased the lawman's number of legal kills to twice their true sum. To punctuate the overstatement, he added, "Marshal Spencer has been known to carry out the will of the people without hesitation. His sight down the barrels of both rifle and revolver are beyond comparison, being deadly with either weapon, and his expertise with a coil of hemp, when fashioned into a slipknot at one end with the other thrown over a limb of a tree and tied to its trunk, is quick and decisive, leaving only the most miscreant detractor to kick."

Pinky John Mallory, the initial cause for Pete Spencer's presence in Carthage City, wasn't one of those asked to leave town. The gambler and the lawman were old acquaintances, and neither had reason to object to the other's line of work. In fact, Mallory welcomed Spencer because he knew that with law and order in the town a higher class of sport would sit at his table to test his skill with a deck of cards. For his part, Spencer respected Mallory as an honest professional, and Mallory's flair with a six-shooter, which had proven handy in the past, would certainly be needed if the situation called for additional firepower.

Peace was something Beecher Hay hadn't wanted for Carthage City, at least not until he was in control of the town. When he found that Spencer wasn't a man to be bought, Hay decided that drastic measures were needed. He sent word to the Cass brothers that he wanted their services. Hay was positive they could stir the cauldron enough to brew the tempest into a hurricane.

Dwight Cass was two years older than his twenty-year-old brother Efrem. The siblings weren't particularly fond of the names their parents had given them at birth, so they had shortened them to Dee and Eff, rather innocent appellations which deceived others into believing they were soft touches. Eight men, if they could return from the grave to testify, would swear an oath to the flint Dee and Eff possessed in their soulless bodies.

Both were uneducated, having spent their childhoods working alongside their widower father on eighty acres of Missouri bottomland, and after the old man remarried and their Bible-toting stepmother sought to rectify that discrepancy, Dee and Eff came to the conclusion that they didn't need any book learning to get by in the world. To prove the point, they jumped a whiskey drummer, beat him with wooden clubs, robbed him, and left him for dead in a nearby cave. The peddler lived and managed to make it to the nearest town where he reported the crime to the sheriff. The lawman knew from the victim's description of his assailants who to go after. He rode out to the Cass place and confronted the old man about his sons. The senior Cass agreed to hand them over to the sheriff, but the boys, only fifteen and thirteen at the time, refused to be taken. To accentuate their stand, they murdered the sheriff right in front of their parents, took the dead man's gun and horse, and rode out of Missouri forever.

Their careers as badmen were limited to petty thefts of lone riders and isolated farmhouses for the next two years. Then the day came when they were boosted into the higher ranks of outlawry. The boys were lolling along a roadside waiting for any single stranger to pass by when they spotted a woman driving a buckboard coming their way. She probably didn't have any money, they reasoned, but she was a female. It was a slow day, so a little sport was in order to break the monotony.

"How do, ma'am?" greeted Dee from atop his horse. He and Eff had blocked the road, forcing the lady to halt in front of them.

"Would you mind stepping down from that rig?"

Her black eyes glared within a tanned face at the highwaymen. She had on a man's hat and short coat, but the rest of her was hidden by a long brown dress. She nodded curtly without speaking and obliged Dee's request, but once she was afoot, the woman displayed a Smith & Wesson .38, aiming it at arm's length at the older brother's face.

"Now it's your turn, sonny. Get down from there, but first I want those six-guns. Take them out real gentle and toss them over here."

Dee laughed at her. "Who the hell do you think you are, lady? Belle Starr?"

"Yes." The answer was matter-of-fact and reprimanding.

"For real?" blurted Eff.

"If you boys don't hurry up and mind me, you'll never find out."

"I believe her, Dee." Eff threw down his gun.

"Boy, I'm losing my patience with you," said Belle.

"Okay, lady, you got us," said Dee as he also complied with her command.

"You boys are awfully young for this sort of thing, aren't you?" She gave them a thorough once-over. "I can see by the slack in your jaws that you ain't too good at it either. You best come to my place with me. You can eat, then Sam and me can decide whether you're worth keeping or not."

Belle and Sam Starr were good teachers of the outlaw arts, and Dee and Eff Cass were apt pupils. The brothers would have remained longer in the hills of eastern Oklahoma than the three years they spent there, but a cattle raid that went awry caused them to part ways with Belle. There wasn't supposed to be any killing. Dee and Eff thought differently, so the Starrs sent them on their way.

As their reputations grew, the Cass brothers found themselves in a peculiar position of being wanted by both sides of the law. Sheriffs and marshals in three states and as many territories were eager to put ropes around their necks, and several outlaw gangs wished to enlist them. As they rode about New Mexico Territory, always a day ahead of Pat Garrett, who was sure that they were accompanied by Billy the Kid, word finally caught up with them that Beecher Hay wanted them to get rid of a lawman.

No one in Carthage City recognized Dee and Eff the day they rode into town. Pete Spencer had heard of them, but he had never met them face to face. When he walked into the Golden

Palace that afternoon, he had no idea who he was going up against.

Dee and Eff had been drinking most of the day, but they had been civil most of the time. Two of Louisiana Sal's girls, the twins Elizabeth and Victoria, were helping them down one shot of whiskey after another, and the boys were enjoying the company of the ladies. It was near four o'clock when the Casses decided it was time the women took them up to their rooms. When they were refused, Dee and Eff got rough with Elizabeth and Victoria. George Bemis broke up the quarrel at the point of his Winchester and sent for Spencer.

"What's the trouble here, George?" asked the marshal upon entering.

"These boys want to play too hard," explained Bemis.

"What else are these women for?" Dee smirked.

Without a word, Victoria slapped the outlaw.

Cass, just as quick, retaliated by slugging her with his fist, sprawling her at Elizabeth's feet. As sister helped sister, Spencer stopped any further brawling by whipping Dee across the face with the barrel of his Colt.

"You can't do that to my brother," snarled Eff. He lunged at Spencer, but the marshal deftly rapped the younger Cass in the exact same manner as he had the older. With both brothers on the floor, Spencer bent down to relieve them of their weapons.

"Give me back my gun, you bastard!" swore Dee, his voice low but steady as he sat up holding a hand to the gash below his left eye, attempting to stop the bleeding.

"Gladly," Spencer grinned.

He grabbed Dee by his shirt front and jerked him upright. The marshal jammed a knee into the outlaw's groin, then, as Cass doubled up from the blow, Spencer creased the other side of Dee's face with the business end of the Colt. Dee dropped to the floor again, but this time he was unconscious.

"You want yours back, too?" Spencer asked Eff.

"You sonofa —"

The toe of Spencer's boot caught Eff squarely on the chin. Like his brother, he too was knocked into oblivious sleep.

"George, will you give me a hand with this trash?" asked Spencer.

The marshal and the saloonkeeper carried the brothers out to the street where they draped the outlaws over their saddles. Spencer paraded them for all the town to see, then led them out of Carthage City.

Two nights later, just as Louisiana Sal was in

the second chorus of the first song of the evening, a volley of pistol shots and two shotgun
blasts were heard throughout the town. Sal
stopped singing, and everyone in the Golden
Palace listened to whatever it was they expected to hear next.

CHAPTER 11

"The marshal's been shot!" came a cry from the street once silence had stunned the town.

That was all it took to empty every saloon in Carthage City. Miners, businessmen, bartenders, dance-hall girls; everyone poured into the boulevard. The noise from their commotion drowned out the sounds of fleeing horses' hoofs. Anxious talk and questions filled the night air.

"Who did it?"

"Did anyone see who shot him?"

"Where'd they get him?"

"How many of them were there?"

"I didn't see a thing."

"Shot him in the back."

"Never even cleared leather."

"He was a good man."

"Let's go after them!"

"Hold on there," shouted George Bemis

above the pandemonium. "Who are you going after? We don't know who did this."

"It was those two boys the marshal whipped the other day," said Deke McCatty. "It had to be them. I heard them say they were going to get the marshal for that job he did on them."

McCatty had heard no such thing, but the growing, angry mob wanted to believe him all the same.

"I heard them say it, too!" shouted Frank White. "Said they were coming back here to get the marshal, that's what they said."

Bemis had seen people react this way before, and he knew there was nothing that could stop them, with the exceptions of time or an army bigger than theirs. He simply shook his head and walked back to the Golden Palace.

"Where's Russ Nichols?" asked McCatty. "He's the head of the vigilance committee. He ought to be here."

"We don't need Nichols," asserted Wilbur Hodge. "The mayor's here. He can lead the way."

Mordecai was pushed to the front. He avoided looking at Spencer's bloody remains.

"How about it, Mordecai?" demanded Hodge. "Are you going to lead us or do we get a new mayor who will?"

The faces surrounding the journalist wanted

revenge, as did Mordecai, but he felt he wasn't the man to ride the point of this stampede. He, more than any man there, wanted to know where Russ Nichols was at that very moment. Nichols should have been there, but he wasn't. Mordecai was, and he wished he wasn't. As Hodge's threat echoed in his ears, Mordecai made a decision.

"Get your guns, boys!" shouted Mordecai. "Every man with a good horse should meet me in front of my office in five minutes. Is Jack Eldon here?"

"Right here, Mordecai," spoke up the liveryman.

"Jack, get my horse saddled for me, and bring it around to my office."

"Sure thing, Mordecai."

"Okay, the rest of you boys start searching the town. The outlaws could still be around." He glanced down at the marshal's body. "Someone take care of the marshal."

Without waiting for further instructions, the men scattered in all directions at once. Louisiana Sal and her girls took charge of Spencer's corpse. Mordecai scurried for his office.

It took the posse more than the five minutes Mordecai had allotted to assemble. Mounted on horses and mules and carrying all sorts of weapons, they waited for Mordecai to lead them on the chase. The journalist came out of the newspaper building and scanned the faces of the men.

"Any sign of the murderers in town?" asked Mordecai.

"They're long gone, Mordecai," said McCatty.

"Okay, boys," said Mordecai after mounting his horse, "let's ride."

A full moon in the cloudless sky allowed the riders to see the road clearly as they raced down the mountain to the valley. Mordecai wasn't much of a horseman, but his mount was urged ahead by those behind. The little news-paperman soon found that the animal beneath him was in command, and he held on for his life.

When the posse reached the fork where the road split in three directions, one each to Lordsburg, Silver City, and Tombstone, Mordecai managed to halt the mare. He turned her around to face the men he was leading. It was decision time.

"Okay, boys," began Mordecai, "we'll have to divide our forces here. There's no telling which way they've gone. I'll take the Lords-burg road. Hodge, you take some men toward Silver City, and White, you take a bunch toward Tombstone. If you don't find any sign of them by noon, turn back and meet here. Whichever group isn't back by sundown, that's the one who has a track on them. Okay, let's move."

Mordecai was hoping that one of the other posses would find the outlaws, but as luck would have it, when the sun rose, it was plain to see that their quarry was less than a mile ahead of them. The discovery spurred the citizens of Carthage City into hotter pursuit.

The Cass brothers dismounted at the edge of a tributary to the Gila River. Leisurely, they drank from the stream, as did their horses. Once their thirsts were quenched, they walked across the creek but got no farther than the other side.

Seeing the Casses at the waterway, Mordecai divided the men into three groups. He sent two of them in opposite directions to circle around the outlaws. He slowly brought up the third behind the brothers. When he felt they were close enough, Mordecai had his bunch dismount and move in on foot. As soon as he saw that the other members of the posse were in position, Mordecai challenged the desperadoes.

"Hold it right there!" shouted Mordecai as he knelt behind a large rock. "You're surrounded, so throw down your weapons and surrender peacefully."

Dee and Eff cleared their holsters and dropped to their knees at the first sound to reach their ears. They searched the area for targets but could see none.

"I'm the mayor of Carthage City, and you boys are wanted for the murder of our marshal."

"We didn't kill your marshal," replied Dee, "but I sure as hell wish we had."

"That won't do, boys," shouted Mordecai. "We know you did it, so give up now. We'll take you back to town and give you a fair trial."

"The hell you say," retorted Dee. "You've already made up your minds that we're guilty. If you want us, go to fighting. That's the only way you can take us."

Before Mordecai could make another reply, a burst of gunfire exploded to his left. The Casses returned the action, and the battle was on. The concealed posse had the advantages of position and armaments. Using rifles from behind rocks and trees, they had the higher ground on the outlaws, who were limited to handguns and an open space along the creek. Within minutes, Dee and Eff were both wounded and unable to continue the fight. Discovering this, the posse moved in.

Oddly, the brothers had near identical

wounds. Both had been shot in their gun hands, left shoulders, and a knee each. None of the injuries could be termed fatal.

"You boys should have surrendered peacefully," said Mordecai as he clucked his tongue at them. "Now you're going to be in pain all the way back to Carthage City."

"We're not going to take them back to town," said Deke McCatty.

"Yes, we are," rebutted Mordecai.

"Sorry, Mordecai, we've already made up our minds." McCatty pointed to Julius Heintz, who was fashioning a pair of nooses from two ropes he had brought along for the occasion. "We're going to string them up right here and now."

"We can't do that," protested Mordecai. "These men deserve a fair trial in a court of law."

"Save your breath, shorty," winced Dee. "You might as well hang us now as later. Hell, what's the difference. I hurt so much that I think I'd rather get it over. How about you, Eff?"

"Can't fight no more," hissed the brother. "Might as well be dead."

"You heard him, shorty. Ain't going to make no difference to us. Like I said, we didn't kill your marshal, even though that was what we came to town to do. But, hell, you won't believe us. So you might as well get it over."

"I won't have any part in this," said Mordecai flatly.

"Have it your way, Mordecai," said McCatty. He nodded at a few of the other men, who picked up Dee and Eff and put them on their horses. Heintz slipped the loops around their necks, and the outlaws were led to a nearby cottonwood. The ropes were thrown over a strong limb of the tree and tied down to the trunk.

"Make your peace," said McCatty.

Dee struggled to look at his brother. "Wonder who we'll meet in hell, Eff. Kind of wish we was going the other way. I'd like to see our mother again."

"Me, too, Dee." He blinked away a few tears. "Who knows? Maybe we'll get a pardon."

The brothers started to laugh, but the tension of the nooses around their throats cut them off as the horses were chased from beneath them. They naturally fought against the strangling line, but nothing they could do was going to stop the hemp from doing its job.

With horror in his heart, Mordecai watched the Cass brothers die. Voices echoed around him, but he didn't hear a word they were saying.

"I wonder who they were?"

"Called each other Dee and Eff."

"I once heard of a couple of brothers named Cass who went by those letters."

"Do you reckon we hung the Cass brothers?"

"Probably was them."

"Yeah, probably was."

"Come on, Mordecai. Let's head on back. We're all done here."

Mordecai stood frozen.

Deke McCatty touched his shoulder. "Let's go, Mordecai."

"We can't leave them up there," whispered Mordecai as he stared at the two bodies swaying in the breeze. "We have to bury them properly . . . with prayers . . . and all."

McCatty polled the others with his eyes. They were sympathetic to the mayor's request. As Mordecai sat by and watched, two holes were dug for graves and the brothers were laid to rest. The shock of the incident was wearing off and Mordecai overheard a conversation between two men holding the horses.

"I wonder if we caught the right men."

"Of course, we did."

"I'm not so sure."

"And why not?"

"Did you feel their horses?"

"No, why?"

"They wasn't even sweated. Two horses that had run most of the night and half the next day would be sweated."

"But they weren't. Humph! That is a wonderment."

Not to Mordecai it wasn't. They had hung innocent men – innocent of Pete Spencer's murder, that is. Only the knowledge that the journalist garnered about the Cass brothers and their notorious deeds salved his conscience in the days ahead. They had deserved to die, he reasoned, but he was sorry that he had been a party to the lynching.

The real murderers of Pete Spencer escaped the wrath of the posse, but the demise of the Cass brothers blooded the citizens of Carthage City. They would no longer tolerate violence in their community, and they served notice of their decision by advertising in the *Clarion* and the *Leader*. Every hardcase in the territory was warned that they would be thrown a necktie party if they should come to Carthage City intent upon disturbing the peace. The admonition was given strength within a week after the caution was made public.

Two circumstances gave rise to the event. Russ Nichols had been absent the night the marshal was shot down, and no one had seen him since early that day. A fortnight had since passed, but before a week had faded from the calendar, tongues began to speculate on the prospector's fate.

Mordecai, more than any man in the vicinity, was greatly concerned for the welfare of his friend and benefactor. He openly questioned everyone with whom he came in contact about Nichols, and the inquiries served to increase the curiosity of others. Mordecai suggested a search be made for the missing miner, but there were no takers. Gradually, the journalist came to the conclusion that Nichols was dead.

The other fact which aroused suspicion among the townspeople was the rather sudden friendship between Beecher Hay and Pinky John Mallory. The mining executive seemed to be in constant accord with Mallory as they drank and played cards together. The association went unnoticed in the beginning, but gradually it became the subject of whispered conversations, then open talk. It took Louisiana Sal to point it out to Mordecai, and once she had, the journalist began adding up the obvious and came out with a minus sum.

Mordecai reasoned, and in print no less, that Russ Nichols had only two enemies within all Carthage City. Beecher Hay because of the conflict over the mines, and Pinky John

Mallory because of the fistfight over Mordecai. Hay and Mallory were now apparent friends, and Russ Nichols was missing. Could Hay, Mordecai asked rhetorically in the *Clarion*, have employed Mallory to removed the major obstacle to his goal? And did Mallory carry out his employer's wishes willingly, as he also had reason to be rid of Nichols?

The answers to those questions were discussed in every saloon in town the afternoon the *Clarion* was distributed.

Beecher Hay read Mordecai's editorial and immediately realized that his neck was on the line. He left town before the beer and liquor being poured so freely down the throats of the miners could take an evil effect.

For Pinky John Mallory, it was business as usual. He had read the insinuating commentary, but he chose to ignore it, feeling that he could ward off any trouble that might arise from Mordecai's words.

Although there was absolutely no evidence that Russ Nichols was dead or that the gambler had been involved in the alleged murder, the groups of men huddled about the bars of the town allowed their shots of rye and glasses of lager to convince them that there was reason to suspect foul play. By sundown, the jury was in and Pinky John Mallory and Beecher Hay were convicted of doing away with Russ Nichols.

"Let's string them up," slurred Deke McCatty. "We should have done it long before now, so let's not waste another minute. Someone get a rope."

That was all it took to start the riot. The word was quickly passed from jughouse to watering hole, up and down the street, and the boulevard filled with men.

The crowd in the Golden Palace, which included Mordecai, had Mallory backed against a wall. The gambler had both his .45 and derringer cocked ready to kill the first man to come toward him.

"Hold on there!" commanded George Bemis from behind the bar. He had his Winchester primed and aimed. "There won't be any lynching in my saloon."

"We don't plan on doing it in here," said McCatty.

"That's right, George," confirmed Wilbur Hodge. "We're going to take him outside to string him up. Ain't that right, boys?"

A cheer of agreement went up.

"I don't care," countered Bemis. "You aren't going to hang that man. He hasn't done anything that we know of."

"He killed Russ Nichols, didn't he?"

argued McCatty.

"We don't even know that Russ is dead," rebuked Bemis.

"If he ain't," said Hodge, "then how come Hay beat it out of town so fast when he read Mordecai's paper this afternoon? Answer me that, George."

"He probably figured out what Mordecai was trying to stir up," replied Bemis.

"And he was right about that, wasn't he?" Hodge laughed.

There was a chorus of guffaws all around except from Bemis and, of course, Mallory.

"I'm warning you, boys," said Bemis. "You're not going to take Mallory."

No sooner had he said the words than a beer mug crashed into the side of his head, knocking him senseless long enough to allow a couple of men time to disarm him. The mob was then able to turn its full attention on Mallory.

"Okay, gambling man," said McCatty, "it's your turn."

"One step, McCatty," warned Mallory, "and you're a dead man. I've got seven bullets in these guns, and that means I can kill seven of you before you can get me. Which seven is it going to be?" The lynchers were silent. "Aw, come on, boys. Let's have some volunteers. I'm not particular about who I have to take to hell with me, so step right up."

No one moved. It was a Mexican standoff for the moment but not much longer than that. Some shouts from the street distracted Mallory's eyes for a single blink, and the instant was used by Frank White to hurl a whiskey bottle at the gambler. The missile struck him in the right hand, jolting his six-shooter from his grip. The collision rocked Mallory off balance, and McCatty seized the opportunity to grab him. There was a brief struggle and a harmless gunshot, but the miners soon had Mallory bound and gagged.

"Okay, boys," announced McCatty, "we got him now. Let's string him up."

Without further fuss, four men hoisted Mallory into the air above them and allowed the crush of the mob to carry them outside, but the sidewalk was as far as they went.

"What's going on here?" demanded Russ Nichols as he stepped out of the crowd in the street.

Mordecai recognized his friend's voice even though the haze of alcohol which was clouding his senses. He squirmed through the human mass to greet Nichols.

"Russ, you're alive!" wept Mordecai, real tears induced by intoxication and emotion streaming from his eyes.

"Of course, I'm alive," said Nichols. He looked at Mordecai, and suddenly everything that was happening became very clear to him. "You mean, you thought I was dead?"

"Well, weren't you?" cried Mordecai. "But now you're alive, aren't you?"

"Yes, Mordecai, I'm alive." He patted Mordecai on the shoulders as he gazed past the journalist. "What's going on here, McCatty?"

"We thought you were dead, Russ," stammered McCatty. "We thought someone had killed you, and . . ."

"And you thought Mallory did it. I see, and you were going to make Mallory pay for my death. Is that it?"

"Well, sort of," said McCatty.

"Put that man down!" shouted Bemis from within the saloon.

"You heard George," said Nichols. "Put him down."

Mallory was lowered to the boardwalk and left in a sitting position, hands and feet tied and a neckerchief crammed into his mouth. Nichols moved over to him and removed the gag.

"Thank you, Nichols," rasped the gambler.

"Save it, Mallory. I would have done the same for a cur. I still don't like you, but never let it be said that Russ Nichols would let an innocent man die."

"I'm still grateful, Nichols."

Bemis worked his way through the mob, which was quietly dispersing. He knelt on one knee beside Mallory and removed the bindings around the gambler's wrists.

"Thank you, George. For this and for what you tried to do inside."

"I try to keep a cool head on my shoulders, Mallory."

"What's been going on around here, George?" asked Nichols.

"This is your fault, Russ," accused Bemis. "If you hadn't disappeared, none of this would have happened."

"Well, I'm back now."

"Where have you been?" asked Bemis.

"Hunting."

"Well, why in hell's name didn't you tell someone where you were going?"

"It was no one's business but my own." Nichols scanned the area. "Where's the marshal? Why wasn't he here to stop this?"

"Pete Spencer is dead," said Mallory.

"And so are those two cowboys he pistol-whipped," added Bemis. "Mordecai led a posse after Spencer's killers, and they caught up with the Cass brothers, the boys Spencer beat on. Posse lynched them down in the valley."

"I tried to stop them, Russ," said Mordecai at his side. "Honest, I did."

"I believe you, Mordecai," said Nichols.

"It might have been different if you'd been here," said Bemis. He stood up, then helped Mallory to his feet. "If you'd been here, Mordecai wouldn't have had to lead the posse. You would have done it, and maybe you could have stopped the lynching."

"Well, he stopped this one, didn't he?" insisted Mordecai in his friend's defense.

"That's one for his side," said Bemis.

Mallory held out a hand to Nichols. "I'd like to bury the hatchet, Nichols. I'm grateful that you saved my life."

"Like I said before, Mallory, save it."

"Have it your way, Nichols." He turned to Bemis. "Buy you a drink, George?"

"In a minute, Mallory. First, I've got a few words for our newspaper friend here." Bemis turned on Mordecai. "I know you're not in the best of conditions to understand this, Mordecai, but I want you to hear it anyway. You're as much to blame for this as Nichols is. Just because a man drinks and plays cards with someone you don't like doesn't mean he's cut from the same cloth. If you'd asked me before printing all that hogwash about Mallory being linked up with Hay, you would have found out that Mallory has been making a pretty good living off the old coot."

"That's right," concurred Mallory. "Hay asked me to work for him, but I refused. I don't like the man, but I feel sorry for him. No one in town would talk to him but me, and my only interest in him was lifting some of that cash he's got at my poker table. Nothing more and nothing less."

"But why did Hay leave town?" asked Mordecai.

"You scared him off with that editorial," said Bemis.

"That's right," agreed Mallory. "He warned me to get out, saying that you were trying to get my neck stretched as well as his. He was damn near right. Hay may be gone for the moment, inkslinger, but he'll be back."

CHAPTER 12

Mallory proved to be correct in his prediction that Beecher Hay would return to Carthage City. The mining executive was accompanied by a host of men, ostensibly construction workers for the building of the stamp mill, but on a closer inspection, the scrutinizing eye could discern that some of the so-called laborers were actually gunslingers. This fact escaped Mordecai's attention.

Bold as brass, Hay visited Mordecai at the *Clarion* office soon after he was settled in the Golden Palace Hotel. Since Hay had only Sven Ulven with him, Mordecai felt secure in his surroundings, but as an insurance against any potential violence on Hay's part, he left open the desk drawer containing the Remington .25, placing the gun within easy reach.

"Mr. Courtney, I've come under a flag of truce," said Hay as he stood in front of the journalist's work area. "For the time being, I'm going to forget the unkind words you've printed about me."

"That's very generous of you, Mr. Hay," said Mordecai, "but I hope you don't expect an apology because none will be forthcoming. However, to prove myself the equal, I'm willing to overlook that fanciful tale you helped Mr. Wooley weave about Carthage City in the *Leader*."

"Very good, sir." Hay smiled. "Then we can proceed with business. Of course, you know my engineer."

"Mr. Ulven, isn't it?"

"Yes, sir," said Ulven with a nod.

"It's nice to see you again," said Mordecai.

"As I was saying, Mr. Courtney," interjected Hay, "now we can continue the business which brought me to this town in the first place. In spite of the obstinate behavior of Mr. Nichols and the other miners, I feel that Southwest should proceed with the building of a stamp mill. Thus, you see, the reason for the workmen who have arrived with me this day. Mr. Ulven has selected a site for the mill, but there, sir, is the rub. The proposed location is on land owned by Mr. Nichols, and I know that you have the legal powers to dispose of the property. Is that not so?"

"Quite correct," said Mordecai. "And you are even more correct about the point that it is a contention. Mr. Nichols, who is my very good friend, has entrusted me with his property, but he has the final say on any transactions."

"And you feel that he would block any sale of land to Southwest?"

"Not necessarily," said Mordecai. "If you can show good reason for placing the mill on his property, a reason which would, say, benefit all concerned, especially the miners, then he might be persuaded to part with the real estate."

"I see." Hay nodded seriously. "Sven, I think you should explain to Mr. Courtney why that particular lot is essential to our plans."

"Yes, sir," said Ulven. "Mr Courtney, do you know anything about geology?"

"I'm afraid the subject is completely foreign to me," admitted Mordecai.

"Well, sir, I'll try to explain as simply as I can," began Ulven. "You see, Mr. Courtney, this particular area is full of faults, and . . ."

"I know it isn't ideal," interrupted Mordecai, "but . . ."

"No, sir, you don't understand," continued Ulven. "A geological fault is a crack in the earth. These cracks make the land very unstable."

"How do you mean?" quizzed Mordecai.

"The potential for landslides is very high. If an explosive should be detonated in the wrong place, it could start an avalanche."

"I see," said Mordecai, "but what has this got to do with building a mill?"

"A stamp mill, Mr. Courtney, is a very large structure, and crushing ore requires a tremendous amount of power. The force of the stamps is very strong, so the mill has to be built on solid foundation. The only area large enough and stable enough for the mill is located on the north side of town, but I have my doubts about that place, too."

"There's no need to go into that," said Hay. "As you can see, Mr. Courtney, we do have a problem here. The miners need to have their ore crushed and smelted, and we need a place to build our mill. Now if you can prevail upon Mr. Nichols to see how everyone can benefit from Southwest building a mill on that spot, then we can proceed, and Carthage City can move forward."

"I'm all in favor of that, Mr. Hay. I agree with you wholeheartedly that a mill is definitely in order. I give you my word, I will do my utmost to persuade Mr. Nichols of the virtue of having the mill constructed exactly where you want it and as soon as possible."

Hay was all smiles. "Very good, sir." He offered his hand to seal the bargain. "I hope we can start anew and let the past be forgotten."

Mordecai reluctantly accepted the handshake. "Yes, it is time to move ahead with the growth of Carthage City."

The mining men departed, and Mordecai locked up his office before hurrying down to Jack Eldon's livery stable. He had young Eldon saddle his horse, and he rode up to the Lucky Nickel to visit Russ Nichols.

The miner was working outside when Mordecai arrived. He sat down on a pine log near the shaft entrance as the journalist dismounted.

"Well, Mordecai, what brings you up here?"

"Beecher Hay," said Mordecai matter-of-factly.

"Oh, yeah? What is that snake up to now?"

"Now, Russ, I think we should have an open mind when dealing with Mr. Hay. After all, the man is only looking out for business."

"Hay finally bought you out, is that it, Mordecai?"

Mordecai reacted as if he had been slapped in the face. His eyes widened, then fluttered in remonstrance.

"Russ, you could have kicked me a little harder, couldn't you?"

"You haven't answered my question, Mordecai."

"No, I have *not* sold out to Hay. I have had a meeting of minds with him, however."

"Yeah, I'll bet."

"Your sarcasm is totally unnecessary, Russ. Please keep an open mind. What I have to discuss with you is of the utmost importance, not only to you and me but to everyone in Carthage City."

"Okay, Mordecai," sighed Nichols as he relaxed on the log, "let's have it. What earth-shaking deal have you made with Hay?"

Mordecai broke into a laugh.

"What's so funny?"

"Your choice of words often amazes me, Russ. Let me explain, and you'll see the humor of it."

Mordecai recounted the conversation with Hay and Ulven in his office earlier that day, and Nichols listened and weighed every word of it.

". . . so you see, it is imperative that we sell the lot to Hay."

"I agree," said Nichols.

"You do?"

"Of course, I do. Do you see all that ore over there? A lot of good it's doing me sitting there. I can get a little gold out of it, enough to meet my needs, but if I want to get out of here and buy that ranch I want, that ore has to be crushed and melted down. I may not like Hay, but just like every other man up here who's got ore piling up, I need him. You go ahead and sell him that lot. Give it to him if you like, but turn it over to him immediately so he can start building that mill."

Mordecai grabbed the prospector's right hand in both his and shook it vigorously. "I'm glad to hear you talk like that, Russ. Everyone in Carthage City will be delighted as I am to hear the news."

"I still don't trust Hay," said Nichols, as he pried himself free of Mordecai's grip. "He still bears watching."

"Don't worry about Hay. We've got him in our corner now."

"Yeah, I'll believe that when hell freezes over."

Mordecai said farewell and mounted his horse. As soon as he had the animal back at Eldon's livery, he rushed about town looked for Beecher Hay. He found him sitting in the Bonanza Room drinking with Sven Ulven and another character Mordecai didn't know yet.

"Ah, Mr. Courtney," said Hay magnanimously, "won't you join us for a drink? On me, of course."

"The pleasure is all mine," said Mordecai as he pulled up a chair. He let Hay order another round before entering the conversation. "I have good news, Mr. Hay."

"Mr. Nichols has given his consent?" guessed Hay.

"Precisely." Mordecai smiled.

"Never mind the whiskey!" Hay shouted to Bemis. "Bring us champagne! We have reason to celebrate. In fact, set up champagne for the whole house and bring the bill to me."

The gesture was generous but only on the surface. Hay was quick to count heads and found that there were only eight other patrons in the Golden Palace.

The celebration continued throughout the afternoon as Hay continued to buy drinks for every man who entered the barroom. As the sun went down, the bargain was struck between Hay and Mordecai for the purchase of the lot. Hay paid the nominal sum of $500 for the parcel of land, and Mordecai immediately spent part of the cash for another round of champagne for the whole house.

During the whole time Mordecai sat at the table, he never once asked Hay about the stranger who was sitting with them, and neither Hay nor Ulven volunteered to introduce the third man. Oddly enough, Mordecai

never noticed that the man remained silen
during the entire time he was there. Th
journalist was simply too happy to care.

Pinky John Mallory cared. He knew this nev
fellow with the dark eyes, one of which wa
cocked to the side. His hair had gained a fev
touches of gray since Mallory had last seen hin
in Denver, and he walked a little slower anc
maybe not as straight. He no longer wore th
leather vest and chaps of a cowhand, bu
the black suit couldn't hide the steel body
within it. He still carried the same silver
plated, scroll-engraved Smith & Wesson
American .44 with the ivory grip. The
handgun was Jack Maler's trademark, anc
Mallory was quite aware of the killer's
expertise with the piece.

Denver, in comparison to other western
cities, was sedate. Most of its wild days were
behind by the time Custer met his fate at the
Little Big Horn. The shoot-outs in the streets
were gone, and the raucous revelry of cowboy
fresh from a long drive were no longer
tolerated by the city's police force. To be sure
men still carried guns and there was ar
occasional gunfight, but the violators were
promptly hauled off to jail to face trial
whether the shooting was justified or not.

Maler was the first of a new breed infesting

the West. It wasn't his style to face a man in the street or across a barroom floor. He did his killing from behind, in the dark of night, or on a lonely byway where no one could witness the outrage. No one had ever proven a murder allegedly committed by Maler, but those men who inhabited Denver's Tenderloin District, especially those who frequented the gaming houses along Holladay and Blake streets, knew that Maler was a cold-blooded killer, a man to be feared when he wasn't in plain view.

Mallory was peacefully playing cards one day in the Colorado city. Also at the table were George Devol, a tinhorn from the East named Beckwith, and Maler. Mallory and Devol, both professionals at the game, were barely breaking even, but Maler was losing consistently as Beckwith raked in every other pot. As the evening progressed, Maler began making remarks about Beckwith's luck, often insinuating that the easterner seemed to be having more than his share of good fortune. Finally, Beckwith had heard enough. He openly challenged Maler to call him a cheat and then go to fighting, but Maler declined. Morosely, Maler left the table. Mallory, Devol, and several others advised Beckwith to leave town posthaste, explaining the danger in which he had placed himself. Wisely, the gambler took the night train to Kansas City. No one noticed Maler's absence from the city. A week later the *Rocky Mountain News* reported that Beckwith's body had been found alongside the railroad tracks just inside the Kansas line, a bullet in his brain, his clothing picked clean of wallet and jewelry. Maler showed himself that same day wearing a stickpin that bore a striking similarity to the one Beckwith had owned, and when the gunman sat down to play that evening, he had a very large bankroll.

Although everyone knew that Maler had more than likely been Beckwith's killer, the murder meant nothing in Denver because it had apparently occurred in another state. Kansas lawmen paid little attention to the crime, and the railroad detectives couldn't be bothered with it because they were too busy trying to catch train robbers who were stealing the line's money. Besides, there were no witnesses.

Now Maler was in Carthage City and in the company of Beecher Hay. Mallory didn't like the smell of it, and he decided a warning should be put out to the right people. The next morning he was in Mordecai's office.

"Mr. Courtney," said Mallory as politely as he could, "I know you don't particularly care for me . . ."

"An understatement if I ever heard one," sneered Mordecai.

The gambler straightened his back as he stood next to the journalist's desk. His eyes pinched together, and his breath hissed into his lungs. For a second, he forgot why he was there, but he quickly regained control of his emotions.

"For the moment, little man," growled Mallory, "let's put the past aside and consider the present."

Mordecai quietly slid open the top drawer of the desk and slipped his hand inside. It found the Remington.

"Speak your piece, Mallory, and have done with it."

"Last week you were worried about my association with Hay," began Mallory. "You've since learned that I won't have any truck in his schemes. This week you do have reason for concern."

"Changed your mind about Hay, have you?"

Mallory smiled, the derisive grin of a wiser man about to chastise the fool. "Hardly, Courtney. I'll continue to take Hay's money at my poker table, but I'll never work for him, no matter what the wage. No, little man, it isn't me that you have to ever worry about. It's Jack Maler that should be keeping you awake at night."

"Who?"

Mallory was incredulous. "Jack Maler, you imbecile."

"Sorry, I don't know the gent."

"You don't know him? You must! You drank with him all afternoon yesterday."

"Oh, you mean the quiet fellow who was with Mr. Hay."

"That's right, inkslinger. His name is Jack Maler."

"Okay, his name is Jack Maler. What about him?"

Mallory shook his head. "Evidently, you've never heard of Maler."

"Can't say that the name means anything to me."

"Well, it will, if you aren't the one he's here to kill."

"What's this?" Mordecai was suddenly all ears.

"Jack Maler is a paid killer."

"How do you know this?"

Mallory spent the next ten minutes relating every detail he knew about Maler to Mordecai. The journalist, as he listened, slowly lost what little color his skin could muster.

". . . and now he's here in Carthage City, and that means someone is going to die soon."

"Can you be sure of that?" asked Mordecai.

"As sure as the sun will come up tomorrow,"

snorted Mallory.

"Why are you telling me all this?"

"I usually don't stick my nose into other people's business, but I don't like killings, especially the kind Maler specializes in."

"That I find hard to believe."

"Well, you just keep believing that, little man," sneered Mallory, "and when you get to the Pearly Gates, tell it to St. Peter."

"How many men have you killed, Mallory?"

"That's a score I don't keep. I don't put notches on my gun, and I don't go looking for trouble like Doc Holliday. At the same time, I won't run when threatened."

"I suppose I should thank you for warning me," said Mordecai.

"Save your breath on that score. Just thank yourself you didn't do anything foolish these last few minutes."

"How do you mean?"

"If you'd tried to pull that gun out of that drawer, you'd be a dead inkslinger right now."

With that Mallory tipped his hat, smiled, and departed, leaving Mordecai to ponder everything the gambler had told him, especially the part about his probable death.

After due consideration, Mordecai made his first move. He went looking for Hay and found him at the site of the proposed mill. Jack Maler was standing next to the mining executive as they watched the workmen clear the lot and dig the foundation trenches.

"Ah, Mr. Courtney," greeted Hay, "how nice of you to come out!"

"Good day, Mr. Hay," returned Mordecai, a forced smile on his lips. "And to you, sir," he added, nodding at Maler.

Maler repeated the gesture but didn't speak.

"With all that ore piling up along the slopes," began Hay, "I could see no reason to delay this project any longer. Besides the mill, we'll be building a road around the canyon so our freight wagons can have easy access to the mines. I've already hired the men and equipment for that job. They should be up here within the week."

"I didn't realize how involved this was going to be," said Mordecai. "Most impressive, Mr. Hay."

"Yes, indeed."

"Excuse me if I appear rude, Mr. Hay, but I don't believe you've introduced your friend here."

"The impropriety is entirely mine, Mr. Courtney," said Hay, still the congenial host. "This is Mr. Jack Maler, my construction boss. Jack, this is Mr. Mordecai Courtney, the publisher of the Carthage City *Clarion*. I believe

I've mentioned him to you."

"Oh, yes," said Maler. Half of his mouth twisted into an evil grin. "Mr. Hay has spoken of you often, Mr. Courtney."

Mordecai offered a friendly although reluctant handshake. Maler accepted it and nearly crushed Mordecai's hand in the process.

"Are you also an engineer, Mr. Maler?" asked Mordecai.

"No, I'm just ramrodding this outfit, if you know what I mean."

"Ahem!" Hay cleared his throat. "Mr. Maler's position is mostly as foreman for the construction crew. It's his duty to see that we don't have any trouble."

"I see," said Mordecai. "Well, I can see that you gentlemen are quite occupied here, so I'll be on my way. Good day."

So Mallory was right about the stranger being Jack Maler, thought Mordecai as he walked toward the Golden Palace. Was he also right about the man's reputation and true occupation? Better do some checking around.

George Bemis was the first man Mordecai cornered and questioned about Jack Maler. Bemis recognized the name and seemed to recall that he'd heard bad things about Maler, but he couldn't remember anything specific.

That was the most information he was able

to garner from anyone until he thought of asking Louisiana Sal. She had known about Hay, so maybe she knew about Maler, too. It wouldn't hurt to ask.

"Jack Maler? Yeah, I know about him, Mordecai. Why do you ask?"

"It's my business to know about everyone," said Mordecai as he leaned back in the chair. "That's how I get my stories."

"Well, Jack Maler is someone you don't want to write about in your newspaper. He's bad news, Mordecai, and you'd be wise to steer clear of him."

"I would? Why?"

"Maler is crazy. He kills because he likes it."

"He's a killer?" Mordecai sounded surprised, as if he hadn't heard that about Maler earlier in the day.

"He's never been caught at it, but everyone knows he's responsible for a lot of men being in the ground."

"You don't say!"

"Take my word for it, Mordecai. Jack Maler is a killer."

That was enough to convince Mordecai that Hay was up to no good. Why else would he have a man like Maler around?

CHAPTER 13

Construction of the stamp mill moved ahead rapidly, and the ore road was completed within a week. Beecher Hay had the freight wagons waiting to haul the rock down to the mill, but there was still the matter of how much he was going to charge the miners for processing their ore.

Mordecai reported the progress of the building as well as the presence of Jack Maler in Carthage City, but he was careful to say that Maler was only there as Hay's foreman. A commentary about men and guns, such as the one he had leveled at Pinky John Mallory, was absent from the *Clarion*. Instead, Mordecai limited himself to the role of peacemaker, saying that it was time for forgetting the past and moving ahead to the future.

Life in Carthage City settled down considerably, even without an official lawman to maintain the peace. The lynching of the Cass brothers by the vigilance committee had much to do with that. Word spread quickly that the better citizens of the mountain community wouldn't tolerate any outlaws in their midst.

The miners, who had once been the great majority in town, were no longer in complete control. Businessmen of all sorts, including Hay, gained the upper hand, and the population became balanced with the influx of construction workers and a number of teamsters. More women arrived, some of a lesser occupation than Louisiana Sal and her girls; others were the wives of men like Harry Willit. There were children, too, which prompted the town council to consider erecting a schoolhouse and hiring a teacher. For all practical purposes, Carthage City was taking on the appearance of a permanent settlement.

The lifeblood of the boomtown was, of course, the gold in the surrounding slope, and the processing and shipping of it were prime concerns for everyone. The key to that end was Beecher Hay, and no one knew that better than he did. Thus, he called the miners together in the Bonanza Room of the Golden Palace to offer them terms for crushing and smelting their ore.

"Gentlemen, if I might have your attention,"

requested Hay from the stage. Jack Maler and Sven Ulven were seated in chairs behind him; Ulven because he was popular with the prospectors and Maler as a reminder that Hay meant serious business. "The last time we met here I made you offers for your properties. We won't discuss the results of that meeting, but I would like to reaffirm those offers." A few groans were emitted from the throats of the more vociferous men in the audience, Deke McCatty in particular. "As I said before, Southwest can offer you no more than the aforementioned sums.

"Now for the current state of affairs. The mill will be ready for your ore in the very near future, as early as next week, I'm told. I'm sure you're all anxious to learn our terms for hauling and processing. The charge for hauling the ore to the mill will be $40 a ton, cash in advance."

"Why, that's highway robbery!" shouted McCatty as he jumped to his feet and shook a fist at Hay.

Several men voiced their agreement but not as openly or as loud. The one man Hay expected to object but who remained silent for the moment was Russ Nichols. He and Mordecai stood in the rear of the hall acting like disinterested spectators.

"I'm sorry you feel that way," said Hay, "but that's the way it has to be. Now if I may continue, the processing charge will be forty percent of the precious metals extracted from the ore. That includes any silver and copper that the ore might contain."

"Hay, you're a thief!" shouted McCatty. "You can take your mill and go straight to hell with it. I'll starve before I'll agree to those terms."

"The same goes for me," said Frank White.

"It's going to be a long, cold winter in these mountains," said Hay. "You men might wish to reconsider. I'll give you ten days to sign a contract. At that time, the charge goes up to $50 a ton."

"Mr. Hay," called Russ Nichols. The sound of his voice silenced the entire hall. "I've already told you what I think of your offer for my mine. Now I'd like to tell you what I think of your present offer."

"Here it comes," said Hay over his shoulder to Ulven and Maler.

"As far as the freight charge goes," continued Nichols, "the money is all right with me, but I have to object to paying cash in advance."

Nichols paused, knowing that some of his friends would question his decision, and they did.

"Are you selling out?" demanded McCatty.

"Throwing in, Russ?" asked Wilbur Hodge.

There were other similar remarks, but Nichols ignored them.

"Cash is something most of us don't have a lot of," Nichols continued. "I've got some, but by the time your men haul my ore to the mill, I'd be broke again. And there's no telling when I'd see any money from the gold in my ore. Now as for you taking forty percent of the precious metals, I think that's a little high, but you do have us over a barrel there. If we want our ore processed, we have to go to you."

"You see things quite clearly, Mr. Nichols." Hay smiled.

"We do have one alternative," said Nichols, more to the other miners than to Hay. "We can build our own mill."

"Hey, that's a great idea, Russ," said McCatty. "What do you say, boys? Do we pay this robber or do we pass the hat and build our own mill?"

To a man, the miners agreed to finance and construct their own stamp mill, and the meeting broke up.

Hay was furious again, but this time he didn't wait for the prospectors to hoot him from the stage. He signaled Ulven and Maler to follow, and the three of them hurried upstairs to Hay's room.

"Close the door, Ulven," ordered Hay as soon as they were inside the apartment. "I was hoping things would be easier, but I suppose we'll have to finish this the hard way. Sven, I want you to ride to the land office in Lordsburg and buy up every parcel of property around this town that doesn't already have a claim on it. In fact, I want you to buy every square foot of soil for a whole mile around Carthage City. Then we'll see where these hooligans build their mill." Hay stared at Ulven, who hadn't moved toward the door. "Get going, Sven. There isn't a minute to waste."

Ulven left the room and followed his superior's orders to the letter. In the meantime, Hay and Maler began working on the remainder of the mining executive's plan.

Since Southwest Arizona Mining Company already owned the best site for a stamp mill, the miners decided to build theirs on the south side of the Carthage City. A delegation was entrusted with the money to purchase the land, and it left for Lordsburg the next day. It never occurred to any of them that Hay might try to beat them to the punch. When the miners' land buyers returned to Carthage City with the bad news, the prospectors met in the Bonanza

Room to decide what they should do next.

"As I see it," said Russ Nichols, "Hay still has us over a barrel. The only place left for us to build a mill is in the valley."

"Then we'll build it there," spoke up Deke McCatty.

"If we do," rebutted Nichols, "how do we get our ore down to it? Hay owns all the freight wagons in this part of the territory, and all the teamsters work for him. Even if we could get the wagons, where are we going to get the men to drive them?"

"Then what are we going to do?" demanded Wilbur Hodge.

"We strike," answered Nichols.

"Strike?" queried McCatty. "How in God's name do we do that?"

"We just keep going on like we did before," explained Nichols. "If we don't give in to Hay, sooner or later he has to offer us more money. He can't afford to keep paying all those mule skinners to sit around doing nothing, and his superiors won't let that mill sit there idle for too long. He'll have to give in."

"What's if it's later?" asked McCatty. "I don't know about you fellows, but I can't afford to keep my ore up on the slope forever. I need money to live on, just the same as everyone does."

There was a rumble of agreement from the audience.

"Listen to me," shouted Nichols to quiet the crowd. "We have to stick together on this. If one of us gives in, we might as well throw in the towel."

"That's easy enough for you to say," said Hodge. "You got money to live on. But what about us?"

"Gentlemen," spoke up Mordecai. Normally, he wouldn't interfere with the miners' business, but this time he was positive that he had a solution to their problem. "Gentlemen, you need not worry about money. I have plenty, and I am willing to loan it to each and every one of you at no interest."

"Why so generous, Mordecai?" asked McCatty, always looking for ulterior motives in others.

"I don't like Hay's treachery any more than you do," replied Mordecai. "What is more, the *Clarion* can only be as successful as the town it serves. If Hay gains control of Carthage City, then I might as well take my press elsewhere."

"That sounds fair enough to me," said McCatty. "What do you say, boys?"

There was a round of affirmative replies from the miners.

"Then it's settled," said Nichols. "We hold

out until Hay comes to our terms."

The next day Mordecai printed the results of the meeting, and he added an editorial about the financial tyranny of Hay. As he spiked Hay's efforts, Mordecai also canvassed the merchants for their support of the miners, asking them to extend credit to all the men with working mines and to lower their prices wherever possible. The journalist penned an anonymous letter to the teamsters in Hay's employ, pleading with them to leave their jobs and side with the prospectors. In vivid words he described how they were aiding the tyrant at the expense of their fellow laborers. Mordecai threw down the imaginary gauntlet at Hay's feet with this open challenge.

As was expected, Hay saw red when the *Clarion* opposed him once again. The time had come, he decided, to put an end to this voice of the miners. Very succinctly, he put it to Jack Maler. "He's all yours."

The Bonanza Room was crowded with revelers that night. Pinky John Mallory had his game open, and Hay was his biggest victim. Louisiana Sal and her girls finished their last number just before midnight, and George Bemis was happily pouring whiskey and beer for a near full house. Maler sat in a corner quietly sipping a mug of lager. As the clock struck twelve, Hay excused himself from Mallory's table and approached the bar.

"Mr. Bemis," said Hay, "I'm in a magnanimous mood this evening. Set up a round for the house on me."

"Sure thing, Mr. Hay," said Bemis. "Next one's on Mr. Beecher Hay," the saloonkeeper announced to his patrons.

"I won't drink on his money," said McCatty.

"Nor will I," said Frank White.

That was the general feeling of the miners who were present, but the teamsters accepted Hay's generosity. Their action didn't sit well with McCatty and his fellows.

"Well, we know who our friends are," sneered McCatty.

"What's that supposed to mean?" inquired a big mule skinner named Ted Ramsey.

"It means you'd drink with a skunk as long as the skunk was buying," replied McCatty. The miner spit into the nearest cuspidor, which happened to be at the wagon driver's feet.

"I don't like your mouth, friend," growled the teamster.

"Your ugly mug won't win any beauty contests either," answered McCatty.

With that, the first punch was thrown, but McCatty, the hardy Irishman whose second nature was to brawl at a moment's notice, repelled the blow.

"You'll have to do better than that," grinned McCatty, and he threw a haymaker that sprawled his opponent against several other freightmen. "Anyone else?"

McCatty shouldn't have asked. Ramsey came back at him, as did several of his friends, and the melee was begun.

Hay had stood by this scene and watched with considerable amusement. As soon as fists were flying, he looked at the corner where Maler had been sitting. Seeing that his employee was missing, Hay smiled knowingly and retired.

While Bemis and his bartenders were doing their best to break up the riot in the Bonanza Room, Maler was hurrying toward the Courtney Building. Hay had told him that Mordecai occupied a room in the rear of the *Clarion*. When he reached the back door, Maler pulled out his American .44, and he tried the knob. It was unlocked. Stealthily, he stepped inside the dark chamber. He could see the bed, but it was empty. He saw the light under the door to the office. Mordecai was working late.

Maler eased his way across the bedroom. He cracked the door and peered into the working area. The journalist was bent over his desk writing. The gunman carefully aimed his weapon at the middle of Mordecai's back, which wasn't completely protected by the chair. An evil grin contorted the killer's features.

Mordecai was totally unaware of the gun being pointed at him. He continued to scratch a few words with the pen. When the line was finished, the strain of bending over the paper nagged heavily at his spine. Seeking relief from the discomfort, he twisted to one side.

Maler fired. The bullet missed its target. Mordecai fell on the floor. Maler threw open the door for a second shot. Mordecai scrambled to his knees. Without stopping to think, he jerked open the desk drawer and found the Remington. Maler got off another round, but this one was prevented from doing the job when it struck the chair. Mordecai turned and aimed the .25 in the direction from which he thought the gunshots had come. He pulled the trigger just as Maler fired a third time. Neither slug hit a man, but Maler's did explode the kerosene lamp behind Mordecai, setting fire to the desk top.

"Maler!" shouted Mordecai as he recognized his assailant. He took deliberate aim at the killer and fired.

The .25-caliber piece of lead caught Maler in the throat just above the sternum. The gunslinger clutched at the wound with his free hand. He staggered backward and bumped into the wall. His .44 spat another bullet but at his feet. Still holding the bloody injury, Maler stumbled through the door behind him.

Mordecai wanted to follow Maler to make certain that the killer was dead, but the heat from the fire demanded his attention. He stuck the Remington inside his waistband to free both hands. He grabbed his coat from the hat tree in the corner and began beating the flames.

The desk was the center of the blaze, but the kerosene had also spilled onto the floor, setting it afire. A stack of old *Clarions* sparked into flames.

Quickly, Mordecai realized that he couldn't fight the fire alone. His coat had ignited, and there was nothing else for him to do but summon help. He ran to the front door, unlocked it, and burst into the street.

"Fire!" he yelled in his high-pitched voice. "Fire! The *Clarion* is on fire!"

A few men who had heard the gunshots of moments before were already running toward the building. Mordecai's urgent cry added speed to their feet, and they also took up the alarm.

Seeing that help was coming, Mordecai

rushed back inside. He wanted to continue attacking the blaze but couldn't. Instead, he went to the press. It, above all else, had to be saved if the fire couldn't be controlled and halted.

More men entered the newspaper office. Some took off their coats and fought the flames. Others began helping Mordecai with the press and the boxes of type. Another filled his arms with bundles of newsprint. Outside, a line formed to pass buckets of water from Courtney Creek to the fire fighters inside. The saloons emptied out immediately, the emergency having a sobering effect on every last man.

The attempt to save the Courtney Building was a futile gesture, but the press and type for the *Clarion* were preserved. The fire fighters did prevent the conflagration from spreading to other structures.

As calm was restored, the questions started. Several men gathered around Mordecai as he sat on the ground next to his few remaining possessions.

"How did it start, Mordecai?" asked McCatty.

"Who was doing that shooting?" asked Julius Heintz.

"Shooting? What shooting?" queried Hodge.

"Take it easy, boys," said Mordecai. "I'll tell you all about it in due time. Right now, I'm more concerned about where I'm going to spend the night."

"I've got a room for you, Mordecai," said Bemis. "I'll put you up at no charge."

"What about my press and type?"

"We'll store it all at my place," said Russ Nichols.

"Thank you, George, Russ. I appreciate it. It's good to know that I have some friends."

Nichols and Bemis exchanged wondering looks.

"What about the fire and the shooting, Mordecai?" asked Nichols.

"All right, if you must know now," grumbled Mordecai. "Someone came in and took a few shots at me. One of the bullets broke the lamp on my desk, and that's how the fire got started."

"Did you see who shot at you, Mordecai?" asked Bemis.

"No," he lied. "I was too busy ducking bullets to take a look at who was sending them my way. I guess the fire frightened him away."

Again, Bemis and Nichols eyed each other. Both knew he was lying, but they also knew there was no sense in pursuing the matter at this point.

Bemis led Mordecai to the Golden Palace, and Nichols called for some men to help him with the printing equipment and materials. The fire out, the other citizens of Carthage City returned to their drinks or their homes.

Upstairs at the Golden Palace, Louisiana Sal took charge of Mordecai. Unknowingly, he had burned his left hand while fighting the fire, and Sal bandaged it as best she could. She washed his face as if he was a child, then turned down the bedcovers for him. She would have undressed him, too, but Mordecai put his foot down there. He dismissed Sal, promising her that he would go straight to bed.

As soon as Sal was gone, Mordecai removed the Remington from his waistband. He checked the cylinder to find that it still contained two unspent shells.

"That should be more than enough," he whispered to himself.

Mordecai went to the door and listened for noises in the hall. There were none. He cracked the door and peeked into the passageway. It was vacant. He stepped outside and crept toward Hay's room. He stopped at the door and tested the lock. The knob turned in his hand, and Mordecai threw open the door.

"It's over, Hay!" growled Mordecai in his toughest voice.

The room was dark, but the light from the corridor illumined the bed. It was empty; Hay wasn't there.

Surprised by Hay's absence, Mordecai began asking himself where Hay might be at that hour. Downstairs in the saloon? More than likely.

Mordecai went to the top of the stairs and scanned the barroom. There were only a few patrons at the bar, and Mallory had closed down his game for the night. A couple of Sal's girls were still drinking at separate tables with two teamsters, but Hay wasn't there.

Again, Mordecai asked himself where Hay might be. The mining executive did have an office at the newly constructed mill. That was the only other possibility. He would have gone there if there was trouble. Mordecai headed for the back stairs to the Golden Palace.

After making certain that the printing equipment was safe, Nichols decided to look in on Mordecai. He entered the saloon and hurried to the bar to ask Bemis where he had put the journalist.

"Maybe you should let him sleep," suggested Bemis.

"Maybe I should, but then again, I'd like to find out what really happened tonight. Aren't you the least bit curious, George?"

"That I am, Russ. I'll go up with you."

Nichols followed Bemis up the stairs to Mordecai's room. The door was ajar and the lamp was still glowing. Mordecai wasn't there, however.

"I knew there was more to this than Mordecai let on," said Nichols.

"Maler?"

"That's what I'm thinking."

"Yes, but where?"

"The mill?"

"Most likely."

"That's where I'm heading, George. Are you coming?"

"Do you need me?"

"Maler is a coward," said Nichols. "I think I can handle him."

"Be careful, Russ."

Nichols nodded and left the hotel by the same exit Mordecai had used.

Mordecai climbed the hill to the stamp mill. His heart was already pounding out a score of extra beats, but the physical exertion taxed his asthmatic lungs even more. He paused outside Hay's office to catch his breath. He wiped the sweat from his forehead with a shirt sleeve. Inwardly, he reassured himself that he was doing the right thing. He entered the mill.

CHAPTER 14

"You are a menace, Hay," spat Mordecai as he faced the mining executive. "You deserve to die. We had a peaceful town here before you came, and now we've got chaos."

Mordecai had surprised Hay. The journalist had thrown open the door to find Hay rummaging through his desk. Seeing the gun in Mordecai's hand, Hay had backed up against a wall, putting the furniture between them.

"Surely, you can't blame these troubles on me?"

"Yes, I can. You hired the Cass brothers to kill the marshal, but they failed. So you brought in Jack Maler to do the job."

"That's preposterous. You know when Jack came to town."

"I know when he came to town in the daylight, but did he come here before that, in the middle of the night? The same night Pete

Spencer was gunned down? What about that, Hay?"

"Look here, Mr. Courtney, I know you're upset over the fire tonight, but . . ."

"That's right, I am, but you see, Hay, I know it was Maler who tried to kill me tonight, and you sent him to do the job. Well, I killed Maler instead, and now I'm going to kill you."

Suddenly, Hay's eyes widened for an instant, then their normal calm of confidence appeared in them. He looked past Mordecai to the door.

"Ah, Mr. Nichols!"

"Russ?" queried Mordecai as he looked over his shoulder.

"Welcome to our little party," said Hay.

"Party?" grunted Mordecai, trying to maintain the rough veneer of the moment. "This is your wake, Hay."

Hay chuckled, rankling Mordecai.

"Put that gun down, Mordecai," sighed Nichols.

"No, Russ, I'm going to kill this bastard."

"No, you're not, Mordecai. If you were going to kill him, you would have pulled the trigger already."

"I wanted to get his confession first," alibied Mordecai.

"What confession?" quizzed Nichols. "Even though we know he's been behind most of the trouble around here, we can't prove it. And even if he did confess to you, it would still be your word against his. Just forget it, Mordecai. Killing Hay won't solve any of our problems."

"Very true, Mr. Nichols," said Hay.

Mordecai lowered the Remington. He appeared dejected, almost as if he was a failure. As a killer, he was.

"Go back to the hotel, Mordecai," said Nichols. "And put that gun away for keeps. I told you before that it would only get you in trouble."

"It saved my life tonight," argued Mordecai. "I killed Jack Maler with it."

"So it was Maler who tried to kill you tonight," said Nichols.

"Jack Maler tried to kill you?" queried Hay for Nichols' benefit.

"As if you didn't know that, Hay," said Mordecai. "Yes, Russ, Maler tried to kill me, but I shot him instead and his body was burned up in the fire."

"This is terrible news," said Hay.

"Only for you, Hay," said Mordecai.

"Never mind that now, Mordecai. Just go back to the hotel and leave Hay to me."

"Okay, Russ, but what are you going to do with him?"

"Mr. Hay and I have a little business to transact."

"Do you mean you're going to sell out?"

"Sell out? No. But I am going to sell the Lucky Nickel."

"You can't do that."

"It's my mine. I'll do with it as I please, and you mind your own business. Now go back to the hotel."

"I don't understand, Russ," said Mordecai softly.

"My little friend, I'll explain it to you someday. Now go."

Mordecai finally left, and as soon as Nichols was positive that the journalist was well on his way, the miner turned his full attention to Hay.

"You're really going to sell?" asked Hay, both surprised and excited.

"Sit down, Hay," said Nichols, ignoring the question. Nichols grabbed the extra chair and straddled the back of it as Hay seated himself. "I'm willing to sell if you'll meet a couple of my terms."

"Let's hear them first."

"You can have the mine for the $5,000 you offered last month, but the ore that I've already dug out of this mountain stays in my possession. You can have your freighters haul it down here, and I'll pay you cash for the charges. We split sixty-forty, just like you offered at the last meeting. Is that agreed?"

"So far so good," said Hay, "but that's only one proposition. What's the other?"

"I want you to stop all this violence. We both know you're responsible for it, but as I said before, nothing can be proven. You stop it, and I'll do what I can to persuade the others to go along with me. I can assure you that they will want the same deal you're giving me."

"We have a deal, Mr. Nichols, but I would like to know why you've had a change of heart."

"Seeing what's happened to Mordecai made me realize that this trouble has gotten out of hand. I want it stopped now."

"I wholeheartedly agree."

"Fine," said Nichols. "Now let's get all this in writing."

The transaction was consummated, and Nichols left the mill for his home. He packed up his prospecting gear, bedroll, canteen, and some canned goods. He wrote a brief note for Mordecai and put it on the press, where the journalist was sure to find it. That done, he departed Carthage City.

After a restless sleep, Mordecai was out o
bed early the next morning. His first order
of the day was to call on Nichols in order to
find out for certain that the miner had sold the
Lucky Nickel to Hay. He knocked on the door
to Nichols' cabin several times but received no
reply from within. Thinking that Nichols had
for some reason gone to the mine, Mordecai
lifted the latch and went inside. Nothing
appeared out of the ordinary to him, as he had
missed seeing the note Nichols had left for
him. Then he thought that Nichols wouldn'
have gone to the Lucky Nickel if he had sold it
On the other hand, he argued with himself
maybe he did for one purpose or another. Mor
decai went to Eldon's livery stable for his
horse.

Nichols wasn't at the mine, but Hay was
Sven Ulven stood alongside his employer as
the two men surveyed the shaft and the surrounding area. As Mordecai rode up, they
broke off their conversation.

"Good morning, Mr. Courtney." Hay
smiled, as effervescent as ever. "I suppose
you're looking for a story for your paper."

"Not really," said Mordecai. "I'm looking for
Russ Nichols."

"The gentleman hasn't graced us with his
presence as yet this day," replied Hay. "I

haven't seen him since we concluded our bargain late last night. I assumed he retired to his home at that time."

"He isn't there either," said Mordecai.

"Then he must be about the town spreading the good word about our transaction."

"Exactly what kind of deal did you two make?" asked Mordecai.

Hay explained the details, including Nichols' promise to persuade the other miners to go along with him.

"I see," said Mordecai when Hay was finished with his narrative. "Well, we'll just keep an eye on the future and see how all this turns out. Good day, Mr. Hay, Mr. Ulven."

Instead of returning to town, Mordecai took the ore road around the slope as he called on the other prospectors at their diggings. None of them had seen Nichols that morning, and every one of them expressed surprise, and some disgust, when Mordecai related to them the facts of the sale of the Lucky Nickel. By the time the journalist had completed the round, the miners were heading to town for a meeting. Mordecai arrived at the Golden Palace just as Deke McCatty was trying to get some order from the men.

"Sit down, and close your yaps!" shouted

McCatty above the din. "I've got something to say, and then everyone else can have a turn if they want one."

Gradually, the jumble of voices subsided and the meeting was officially begun. McCatty stood on the stage and scanned the audience.

"Russ Nichols throwing in," began McCatty, "was a punch in the gut to me, just as much as it was to all of you." A vocal roll of agreement interrupted his speech, and McCatty raised his hands for silence. "Now maybe Russ had good reason for what he did. According to Mordecai, he did it because he wanted all this trouble we've been having stopped. I can believe that. But I can't believe Russ would try to persuade any of us to follow his example. And the reason I can't believe that is I don't see Russ anywhere around here doing any talking to any of us about it. Do you follow me?"

"You're making good sense, Deke," said Frank White from the front row. "Keep it up."

"The way I figure it, Russ wants us to keep holding out against Hay for the time being. Don't ask me why I feel that way. I really don't know. It's just a hunch I got, and I'm going with that hunch. The rest of you can let your consciences be your guides, but as for me, I ain't selling out to Hay until he comes up with a better deal than what Russ got."

"I'm with you, Deke," shouted White.

"Me, too," chimed in Hodge.

A few more individuals added their approval of McCatty's stand, which incited the remainder of the men to offer their support.

Mordecai was pleased by the turn of events. He had been worried that the miners would give up the fight against Hay. An extra edition of the *Clarion* was called for, he decided, in order to aid the prospectors in their struggle.

After checking around town to see if anyone had seen Nichols that morning, Mordecai returned to the miner's cabin to begin work on the newspaper. As he inspected the press for any damage which might have been incurred as a result of the fire or the handling it had received when it was being transported to Nichols' home, Mordecai discovered the note his friend had left for him. He read it with great intent.

Dear Mordecai,

I did what I did for good reason. I can't tell you what that reason is just yet. You will have to trust me on that score. I have gone away for a while, but I will be back. I hope to have good news at that time.

Your friend,
Russ Nichols

So, thought Mordecai, Russ did have an ace in the hole. That explained everything. In the meantime, Hay must be kept in check.

Word of the meeting reached Hay, and when he learned the results of it, he was once again in a fury. Sven Ulven listened to him rave in the mill office.

"I've had my fill of these obstinate dung-diggers," swore Hay. "They have pushed me to the limit. Just when I think we've won, they decide to continue this senseless holdout. I won't stand for it any longer. The time has come for an end to this confrontation.

"Ulven, concern yourself with the Lucky Nickel. I want it totally operational as soon as possible. I want that ore moving down here to the mill on a regular basis. Understood?"

"Yes, sir," replied Ulven.

"In the meantime, I shall do what is necessary for the final stroke."

That evening Hay sat in at Pinky John's poker table, and he was losing as usual. Mallory, however, was not winning. For some odd reason, his mind was preoccupied. Something nibbled at the deep recesses of his brain as if it was trying to escape to his foremost thoughts. When the fight broke out, the idea emerged.

The Bonanza Room was normally crowded after dark, but on this particular occasion, it was more so. When Mallory finally recognized that fact, he sensed danger in the air, and when McCatty began exchanging punches with Ted Ramsey, the same big teamster he had fought before, Mallory knew he would be wise to keep his gun hand free.

George Bemis tried to break up the fistfight before it turned into a real donnybrook, but he failed to do so. Instead, he found himself in the middle of the riot, clubbing his patrons with a bung starter. The more sober ones went down heavily from the blow of the wooden mallet, but those who had imbibed to the limit of feeling no pain were merely annoyed by the banging of the keg opener. Undeterred, Bemis continued to flail away, shouting the whole time for the combatants to restrain themselves, all to no avail.

It seemed that every man in the saloon was involved in the brawl. Hay and Mallory were the only exceptions. There were men on the floor, rolling and wrestling, trying to throw punches at each other but with little success. Chairs and tables were overturned, and bottles and glasses were broken as whiskey, beer, and wine mixed with blood from scraped knuckles and cut cheeks.

Louisiana Sal herded her girls to the staircase, where they both watched the frenzied fighting and defended their position. If a man made a move for the women, he was instantly repulsed by a high kick from Sal's foot. She had seen many such altercations, and at an early age she had learned that no man was going to preserve her honor at such a time. The alternative was to master some sort of self-defense, and the French martial art of sabot seemed to be the most appropriate for a lady of her ilk.

The noise of the fighting attracted participants from other watering holes up and down the street. With each passing second, a new man joined the fray, and gradually the barroom filled beyond capacity. It appeared that the brawl would cease only when no one was left standing.

Suddenly, in the midst of the shouting, name-calling, glass-breaking, and furniture-crashing, a scream was emitted from the high-pitched tonsils of Jeanette, the mulatto girl in Sal's troupe. The shrill cry shocked Sal and the other ladies, and they turned to stare at Jeanette. A look of horror ruled her chocolate face. She pointed to the middle of the gang of fighters. Sal was quick to see what had incited Jeanette to make the outcry.

Knowing that it would be senseless to attempt getting the attention of Bemis or any of the other men, Sal waded into the battle, kicking and shoving with all her strength as she struggled to reach the center of the room. Still, she succeeded, and when she did, she knelt down beside the lifeless body of McCatty, a bowie knife plunged deep into his back below the ribs. She ascertained that the miner was dead, and, in the process, she was smeared with his blood.

A few men around her saw the blood on her hands, and they desisted from further combat.

"Murder!" shouted Sal, and more men, ones who had heard her, halted their belligerent actions. One by one, they encircled Sal and the corpse, each staring with disbelief. Their silence lessened the pandemonious uproar, and Sal repeated the plaintive report: "Murder!"

As noisy as the Bonanza Room had been just seconds before, it became equally quiet. The onlookers hardly allowed a breath among them as they gaped at McCatty's body.

"It's Deke McCatty," whispered White, breaking the lull. Then louder, he added, "He's been stabbed."

"He's dead," said Sal as she came upright.

No one asked verbally who could have committed the crime, but every eye in the room searched those around it for the killer.

"He did it!" exclaimed White, pointing at Ramsey, with whom McCatty had been tangling. "Deke whipped him, so he got revenge!"

White reached for his six-gun, but a bullet fired into the ceiling stayed his hand. The reverberation of the gunshot stunned the entire room into immobility.

"There will be none of that," commanded Mallory. The business end of his Colt was still smoking as he aimed at White. "Just leave that iron in its place."

Mallory was given plenty of room by everyone around him. He stepped up to Sal and offered her a white handkerchief which she accepted in order to wipe the blood from her hands.

"George, I think you'd better get your rifle," said Mallory. As Bemis reached over the bar to retrieve the weapon, Mallory added, "I think the rest of you men would be wise to remain exactly where you are. Any man who moves might as well admit his guilt, and I'll shoot him right now."

Bemis stood up on the bar, the Winchester

cocked and ready. "And I'm backing Mallory's play. I'll shoot the second man who moves."

"Now," said Mallory, completely in charge, "let's find out who owns that Arkansas pig-sticker in McCatty's back. Miss Macomb, is there anything on the handle of that knife that might indicate who it belongs to?"

"If you mean initials or something like that," said Sal, "I didn't see any." She knelt down again for a closer inspection of the deadly blade. "All it's got is a trademark. 'Fine Steel Hunting Knives, St. Louis, Missouri.' That's it, John."

"Thank you, Miss Macomb," said Mallory. "Now, gents, who's going to 'fess up to owning that fine steel hunting knife?" He scanned the crowd, his eyes accusing every man they contacted. "Come now, gents. Someone here owns that knife."

"A knife like that," interjected Bemis, "would have to have a sheath to carry it in. I think all we have to do is search everyone until we find the culprit with an empty sheath."

"You can search me first," said Ramsey. He held up his hands to signify that he was ready for the frisking.

"Gentlemen, if I may interrupt for a moment," said Hay, "I think I have a better solution."

Mordecai entered the premises at that moment.

"What's going on here?" the journalist demanded to know.

"There's been a murder," explained Hay.

"A murder?"

"Yes, Deke McCatty's dead," said White.

"Who did it?" asked Mordecai.

"That's what we're trying to find out," said Mallory.

"As I was about to say," continued Hay," "I think . . ."

"You're probably behind this, Hay," accused Mordecai.

"That's ridiculous!" retorted Hay.

"Is it?" countered Mordecai. "As ridiculous as you sending Jack Maler to kill me last night?"

"Maler acted on his own," answered Hay.

"What are you talking about, Mordecai?" asked Bemis.

"Jack Maler was the man who shot at me last night," explained Mordecai. He heaved his chest. "Only I got him before he could get me."

"You killed Maler?" quizzed Mallory.

"That's right, I did."

"I had nothing to do with it," lied Hay.

"Not much, you didn't," said Mordecai.

"Never mind that now, Mordecai," said

Bemis. "Maler is dead, and we can't prove Hay had anything to do with him trying to kill you. But we can prove who killed McCatty."

"That's right," agreed Mallory. "Now let's start searching people." He turned to Mordecai. "Mr. Courtney, if you would do the honors."

Beginning with Ramsey, Mordecai searched every man in the hall except Hay, because he hadn't been too close to the fighting. Although some of the men had knives exactly like the one that killed McCatty, none of them had an empty sheath. McCatty's killer was still unknown.

CHAPTER 15

After the search, Bemis held an impromptu court of inquiry. Questions were asked, but all the answers were in the negative. No one volunteered any specific facts, although several accusations were made. By the end of the evening, it was apparent that Carthage City was once again divided into two factions: the miners and the teamsters. Some might have said an uneasy peace settled over the town, while others would have called it a temporary truce which was waiting to be broken by the slightest provocation.

The next day McCatty was buried and his mine was sold to the highest bidder, which, of course, was Southwest Arizona Mining Company in the guise of Beecher Hay. With Hay operating two claims, the stamp mill was put into full production. A few men with non-producing shafts decided to take Hay's cash

248

while it was still being offered, and by the week's end, the mining executive was in control of a third of the slope.

With McCatty dead and Nichols gone, the miners were without a leader. They held a meeting in the Bonanza Room to discuss their plight.

"I say we should sell," said White.

"I won't give in," argued Hodge.

That was the divided sentiment of the gathering. The only matter they were agreed upon was unity. If one of the remaining mine owners sold, they would all sell, but the opposite was also true. It seemed they were at a stalemate. Then Mordecai spoke his piece.

"Gentlemen, there is still the alternative of building your own mill. You've already raised the cash for it, so why don't you build it? I know you can't build it up here close to the mines, but you can still construct one down in the valley and ship your ore to it." He raised a hand to stay any interruptions. "Let me finish. I know that Hay has all the freight wagons under contract, but so what? You can transport the ore down on horseback or on mules. Gentlemen, if you have the will to resist, surely you can find a solution to your problems."

"Mordecai's got the right idea," said Hodge.

"Let's build that mill in the valley, and in the meantime, we can figure out a way of getting the ore down to it."

"That's all fine and dandy," said White, "but what about us who have poor claims? We don't have any ore to ship."

"You can work the mill," suggested Mordecai, "and you can do the shipping. There are lots of jobs for all of you. In a sense, you've already made up your minds to start your own mining company, so why not make it legal? That way, you can really fight Hay."

"Say, I never thought of that," admitted White. "Sounds like a good idea to me. What do you say, boys?"

The assembly was in total accord. The miners would form the Carthage City Mining Company immediately.

The news of a rival firm being established in his very midst jolted Hay. When Mordecai jubilantly declared the miners' intention to him, Hay tried but failed to withhold his concern. As individuals, Hay figured he could contend with the prospectors, but as a legally incorporated body with a lawyer to advise them, they would become a formidable foe, one that would not be easily overcome. With that thought in mind, Hay decided the un-written treaty between the miners and the teamsters was due to be broken.

Frank White's claim was adjacent to the one which had belonged to McCatty. Each day since his friend's death White watched Hay's men work the mine. For the first week, White ignored their conversation, but when Ted Ramsey arrived to haul away the ore McCatty had dug from the mountain, White listened intently as the mule skinner jawed with the miners.

"You boys have had your hands full with this one, haven't you?" remarked the teamster.

"Yeah, the fellow that had this place before wasn't much of a miner. I've seen better shafts dug by blind dogs. That fellow couldn't make a straight cut if his life depended on it."

"He wasn't much of a fighter neither," said Ramsey. "He's better off dead."

That pushed White over the edge. With a pickax in hand, he approached his late friend's detractors menacingly.

"Maybe you'd be better off dead!" shouted White as he wielded the ax at the teamster's head.

The mule skinner dodged the attempt and simultaneously lunged into White. The two men tumbled to the ground. White continued to swing the pick, landing an occasional harmless blow. They rolled around in the middle of the road until Ramsey finally came out on top. He pinned White's ax-holding hand beneath one knee, planting the other firmly in the prospector's gut. He crashed a heavy fist in White's face but lost his balance in so doing. White freed the hand grasping the tool, and he instantly swung it at his opponent's head. The point of the ax sunk deep into Ramsey's skull, killing him.

White pushed Ramsey's body off of him. The realization of what he had just done struck him dumb. The blood on his hand and shirt confirmed what his mind didn't want to believe. Anger had prodded him to attack Ramsey, but deep inside, he hadn't wanted to murder the man.

But he had, and the miners working McCatty's claim pointed out the fact to White as they eased their way toward him, shovels, hammers, and picks held threateningly over their heads. White scrambled to his feet and raced for his mine. Hay's men chased after him, but the weapons they carried slowed their pace. White quickly found his Winchester .44 carbine. He wheeled, cocked it, and fired without aiming. The bullet struck a spade. The miners halted their pursuit. White pulled off another round, hitting one man in a forearm. That sent him and his fellows scurrying for cover.

"Run, you bastards!" shouted White. He triggered another shot to emphasize the command.

A fiery storm swept the entire slope and down to the town as the news of Ramsey's death was spread from man to man. As soon as Sven Ulven heard it, while he was supervising the work at the Lucky Nickel, he rode down to the mill to tell Hay.

"There's trouble on the slope," said Ulven breathlessly as he reported to his boss in his office. "One of our teamsters, a man named Ramsey, was murdered by one of the miners."

"One of our people killed Ramsey?"

"No, the friend of the man who was killed in the saloon last week did it. Our men have him pinned down in his shaft."

"Good," said Hay. "Blow the whistle, and get all our men together. We'll take care of this murderer our own way."

Ulven left, and Hay rubbed his hands together with overpowering delight.

"This is working out better than I had hoped," said Hay to himself.

When the stamp mill's steam whistle shrilled steadily, the whole town was alerted. Mordecai, who was close at hand in Nichols' cabin, hurried up to the mill. The first man he saw was Ulven.

"Mr. Ulven, what's the alarm?" asked Mordecai.

"Ramsey, the teamster, was murdered by a miner named White. Mr. Hay is arming the men to go after him."

"He can't do that!" exclaimed Mordecai.

"That's his plan," reiterated Ulven.

"He has to be stopped."

The journalist didn't wait for Ulven to comment any further. He ran back into town and headed straight for the Golden Palace. Bemis and Mallory were standing on the boardwalk looking up the street when Mordecai reached the saloon.

"What's the trouble, Mordecai?" asked Bemis.

Mordecai, his lungs sucking air with every ounce of strength, rasped out the words. "Murder ... Frank White ... killed a ... teamster ... Ramsey ... the one ... McCatty ... fought."

"Great jumping Jehovah!" swore Bemis. "We'll have a war before nightfall if something isn't done immediately."

"I'm with you, George," said Mallory. "Call it and I'll back you."

"Mordecai, where is White now?"

"Hay's men have him trapped in his mine, I guess," wheezed Mordecai.

"How many men?"

"Not many, I think," said Mordecai.

"We'll have to hurry, John. Maybe we can get White out of there before Hay can get his men together."

Bemis retrieved his Winchester while Mallory rounded up three horses. Mordecai regained his breath, and he rushed down to Eldon's for his gelding. Once he was in the saddle, he rode back to Nichols' cabin for the Remington. He joined Bemis and Mallory as they galloped by the house.

Hay's men were still gathering around him at the mill. He and Ulven handed out guns to those men who didn't have one. His employees who were on the slope, with the exception of the handful who were watching White, had yet to arrive. Hay decided to wait for them. He didn't see the three mounted men ride past the mill toward the mines.

Wilbur Hodge was the first prospector to learn about the killing of Ramsey. When he was told that White was responsible for the teamster's death, he began mustering the other miners to support their fellow. They met on the road above White's mine.

When Bemis, Mallory, and Mordecai rode up to where Hay's men were hovered as they kept an eye on White, one of the mining executive's workers stepped from hiding. The riders halted and drew their weapons.

"Hold it right there," ordered Mallory. The man stopped, his hands held high. "Drop your gun."

"I'm not heeled," explained the man. "None of us are."

"Good," said Mallory. "Mr. Courtney, I suggest you go after Mr. White. He knows whose side you're on."

"Quite right, Mallory," agreed Mordecai.

Mordecai urged his horse forward, passing the rest of Hay's men. "Frank White!" he shouted to the prospector. "It's Mordecai Courtney. Come out. We've come to take you back to town."

"You and who else?" called White from within the shaft.

"George Bemis, John Mallory, and myself."

"Then what?" asked White.

"We'll protect you from Hay," said Mordecai as he let his horse walk toward the mine.

"Sounds fair enough to me, but what about those men who are out there now?"

"Mallory has them at gunpoint. It's safe, Frank, but we have to hurry. Hay is arming his men, and they're coming up here after you."

"How are we going to get back to town?" asked White as he emerged from the tunnel.

"We've got an extra horse for you," explained Mordecai, "and we're going to take the long way around and come in from the lower end."

"Then we'd better move," said White.

White followed Mordecai to where Bemis and Mallory were waiting. He climbed onto the mount they had brought for him, and the four men rode off toward Hodge and the other prospectors who were coming their way. In a few minutes, the two groups met.

"You men had better turn around," warned Bemis. "Hay's men are coming up the slope now. If you continue going down this road, you're sure to run into them, and there's no telling what will happen then."

"We're ready for them," said Hodge.

"You can't fight them up here," said Mallory.

"You shouldn't fight them at all," said Bemis.

"It's time we settled the score once and for all," said White. "I settled up for Deke McCatty, but that's only half the battle. Now we've got to take care of Hay. What do you say, boys?"

"We're with you, Frank," said Hodge, and a cheer from the rest of the men confirmed his statement.

"Then let's go after them," said White.

"No, wait!" shouted Bemis. "If you're going to fight, at least give yourselves a fair chance of winning. Hay has more men than you've got here. If you meet him down the road, you're sure to be cut down to a man. But if you follow us on the round-about road, you can make it to town where you'll have a chance to stop them."

"George is right," said Mallory. "You're sure to lose up here. In town, you can put up some kind of defense. But not up here."

"Okay, we'll do it," said White.

As the miners headed for Carthage City, Hay loaded his men into freight wagons and started up the slope for White's mine. Sven Ulven remained behind. A man with education, reasoned Hay, was too valuable to risk in a fight.

Halfway to their destination Hay and his men encountered the miners who had been watching White. Quickly they told how Bemis, Mallory, and Mordecai had rescued White and how the three had taken White the round-about way to town. Hay ordered his men to turn around and return to the mill. From there he would decide how to wrest Frank White away from his friends.

News of the murder and the subsequent events reached Harry Willit at his store. He instantly realized that a fight was inevitable, and he determined, along with the other businessmen of Carthage City, that they would stand aside and let the combatants have it out. They took their women and children and hid behind locked doors and shuttered windows.

Once they were back in Carthage City, Bemis, Mallory, and Mordecai separated themselves from the prospectors. Mordecai thought their action was strange, but he felt the same way when the other two men had decided to go after White in the first place. It was time for some explanation, he told himself.

"Mallory, if I may be so bold," said Mordecai, "what is your stake in this game? You yourself have said that you don't go looking for trouble, but you've seen fit to interfere not only once but twice — last week when McCatty was killed and again today. Why are you doing this?"

The gambler and the saloonkeeper exchanged glances before Mallory made his reply.

"Let's just call it my sense of fair play," said Mallory. "I don't like violence, but I will use it when necessary to mete out a suitable end. If I hadn't interceded last week, there would have been more blood spilled in George's saloon, and I came along today to prevent the same from happening."

"But you haven't yet succeeded today," argued Mordecai.

"True," said Bemis, "but the day is not over."

"You have a plan?" quizzed Mordecai anxiously.

"A feeble one at best," admitted Bemis, "but it will have to do for the moment."

The three men rode past the Golden Palace and made straight for the stamp mill. It was plain for Mordecai to see exactly what Bemis and Mallory had in mind. They had safely guided the miners back to town, buying them time to make a defense, and now they were going to Hay to stall him even more. Possibly, they might head off an engagement through negotiation. It was worth the try, if nothing more. His principles suddenly suffering an attack of capriciousness, Mordecai pictured himself in the role of a statesman sent to mediate the peace between belligerents. It was a lofty view but one not beyond Mordecai's imagination.

Hay and his men arrived at the mill shortly before the three peacemakers. Mordecai immediately noticed the somewhat conspicuous absence of Ulven. He wondered about where the mining engineer might be, but his thoughts were interrupted by Hay's voice.

"What have we here?" demanded Hay. "You've already stolen our prey from us, and now you have the audacious effrontery to confront us with your presence? I find you to be absurd, gentlemen."

Eloquence to Hay, thought Mordecai, must be like a well of cold, sweet water, only to be drawn from when his audience thirsted for the pinnacle of quenching refreshment.

"We acted in the best interests of everyone concerned," said Bemis.

"Not in Ted Ramsey's," cried Hay with a flare of the dramatic. "His cold body lies in that wagon, but his spirit circles around us, urging us on to avenge him, a poor working man struck down by the hand of a bloodthirsty villain."

"What about Deke McCatty?" interjected Mordecai. "What about his body lying in the cemetery and what of his spirit demanding retribution?"

"What of it?" replied Hay simply.

"The point is, Mr. Hay," said Bemis, "McCatty was murdered last week, and Ramsey was the one who most likely killed him. Now Frank White has evened the score by killing Ramsey. Why not let it go at that?"

"Never!" exclaimed Hay. "There was no evidence that Ramsey killed McCatty, but there were several witnesses who saw White plant that pickax in Ramsey's skull. There is the difference, Mr. Bemis."

"Look, Hay," said Mallory, "two men are dead already. If you continue with this hostility, more good men will die. White and his fellows are firmly barricaded in town, just waiting for you to make your move on them. What would you have these men with you do? Sacrifice their lives just so you can hang one man?"

"Yes, I would, because they would be dying in the name of justice."

Suddenly the reality of death loomed over Hay's men, and they searched each other's faces for assurance.

"Justice has already been met," said Bemis. "Ramsey's death for McCatty's. Can't you see that, Mr. Hay?"

Before the mining executive could reply, the arbitrators were interrupted by the arrival of Ulven and Russ Nichols.

"George is right," said Nichols. "That score is settled, Hay, but we have another piece of business which must be finished."

"So you've come back, you scoundrel," said Hay. "We made a bargain, and you failed to uphold your end. Had you done so, all of this could have been avoided."

Nichols glared at Hay. "I held up my end as well as you held up yours."

"But you were the first to withdraw," retorted Hay.

"You could have given me more time," countered Nichols. "But never mind that now. What's done is done. If you would indulge me for a moment in your office, Hay, I believe we can settle this matter once and for all."

Hay cautiously studied the prospector's face before making his decision. With a nod and a wave of his hand toward the mill, he agreed. Nichols followed him inside.

"Hay, I'm going to keep my word," said Nichols when they were alone.

"How so?"

"You still want this slope, don't you?"

"Of course."

"Then let me go into town and talk with the other men. I promise you that before the day is finished, you will have every claim on the slope."

"How do you plan to convince those men to sell?" asked Hay suspiciously.

"I'm going to tell them that I've found a richer strike in the foothills. They'll believe that. Then I'm going to tell them to sell their claims to you. You'll have the slope, and they'll have some money and their lives. Then all these murders will come to an end."

"What will happen to you once they discover you've lied to them?"

"Why are you so concerned about my hide?" countered Nichols.

"Mere curiosity, Mr. Nichols."

"Well, don't worry yourself about me. I'll be long gone before anyone discovers the ruse."

"I see," said Hay. "All right, Mr. Nichols, I'll go along with you for the time being, but if what you promise does not materialize by sundown, I will lead those men outside into town."

"I'll see you later, Hay."

CHAPTER 16

With Sven Ulven's help, Russ Nichols had little trouble convincing the other prospectors to sell their claims to Hay, and by nightfall, Southwest Arizona Mining Company owned the entire slope around Carthage City.

To complete the bargain with Nichols, Hay disarmed his men and ordered them to leave the prospectors alone. When some argued, he threatened them with unemployment at first, then cajoled them by saying his conscience wouldn't permit him to be a part of any more violence and he wished that they would also refrain from further bloodshed. What he didn't tell them, but alluded to in his speech, was how Ramsey had actually been Deke McCatty's killer.

Late that night, Hay and his men filled the Golden Palace as they celebrated the victory over the prospectors. Hay opened his wallet wide and paid for all the drinks. He was happy, and nothing was going to spoil his party. He even had a winning streak at Mallory's poker game. The fact that none of the miners were present in the Bonanza Room completely escaped his notice.

Although he had played cards until well after midnight, Hay was up at dawn preparing to inspect his new properties. He rousted Ulven from his bed and told the engineer that he wanted him to begin operating all the mines as soon as possible. Ulven rolled his eyes, mumbled something that Hay took for obedience, then went back to sleep as soon as the mining executive departed. Hay hurried off toward the stamp mill but was intercepted by Mordecai near Russ Nichols' cabin.

"Good morning, Mr. Courtney." Hay greeted him with a youthful smile. "How are you this fine day?"

"Fit as a fiddle," replied Mordecai. "I'm glad to see you're taking this so well."

"And why shouldn't I? I've finally won."

Mordecai couldn't hold back the laughter. The reaction dumbfounded Hay.

"I'm glad you're happy for me," said Hay uneasily.

"I couldn't be more delighted, Hay. I've waited for this day for a long time. It does me

266

well to see you in your proper place."

"Mr. Courtney, I seem to be missing something here. Would you be so kind as to explain?"

"You certainly are missing something, Hay. Money; all that money you paid Nichols and the other miners for their worthless claims."

"Worthless?"

"That's right, Hay, worthless. Every last one of them. They're all payed out, and now you own a mountain full of giant gopher holes."

Once again, Mordecai began laughing uncontrollably. Hay stared at the journalist as if he was some sort of sideshow freak. Confusion rattled around in Hay's head like seeds in a dried gourd. Gradually, he sorted out what Mordecai had just told him.

"Do you mean . . ."

"You've been hoodwinked, Hay. Russ Nichols has pulled off a colossal trumpery, and you, Hay, are the king of asses, braying louder than ever when *you* are the actual butt of this ocular deception."

"You're mad, Courtney."

"Am I, Hay? Maybe you should have a serious talk with your engineer. Then we'll see who is mad and who is not."

Hay made no reply. He simply turned and walked away toward the Golden Palace,

Mordecai's raucous titter ringing in his ears. The closer he came to Ulven's room, the greater his anger grew.

"Ulven!" screamed Hay as he threw open the hotel-room door, banging it against the wall.

"What is it now?" grumbled Ulven as he rolled over to face Hay.

"Get out of bed, Ulven. I want to talk to you."

"Go to hell. I'm not taking any more orders from you. I quit."

"Quit?" spat Hay. "Then it's true! The mines have payed out."

"That's right, Hay. Oh, there's still some gold in them but not enough to make them profitable for a full-scale operation." Ulven sat up in bed. "Don't look at me like that, Hay. I didn't doublecross you. It was Russ Nichols who deceived you. He told me all about it. His mine payed out weeks ago, but he kept it to himself. As far as the rest of the mines go, none of them were producing that well in the first place. Nichols made them look better than they actually were by salting them late at night when everyone else was drinking in the saloons. I didn't find this out until last night *after* you had bought all the claims."

"Why didn't you tell me all this then?"

"Nichols convinced me not to," said Ulven

'He said you'd probably start all the trouble all over again. Seeing you now, I believe I did the right thing."

"Nichols was right about that, Ulven. I am going to start all the trouble all over again."

"You're too late, Hay. Nichols and all the others are gone."

"Gone?"

"That's right. They pulled out early this morning before the sun came up. They're going down to the foothills to stake new claims."

"Do you mean Nichols really found a new strike down there?"

Ulven laughed. "He told me how you thought he was making that up. My God, Hay, you are easy to fool."

"We'll see who has the last laugh," swore Hay as a parting comment.

"It's too late," shouted Ulven after Hay. Then to himself, he added, "Much too late for you, Hay."

The mining executive rushed out of the hotel without speaking to anyone. He turned up the street and made straight for the stamp mill. He passed Mordecai, ignoring him, too. It was obvious that Hay was determined to reach his destination without delay.

Mordecai entered the Golden Palace. In the

Bonanza Room, he found Bemis on the job despite having worked until a late hour the night before. The journalist stepped up to the bar to converse with his friend.

"Morning, George. Up kind of early, aren't you?"

"There's no time to lose, Mordecai."

"Then you've heard the news?"

"That's right. Hay was upstairs a few minutes ago talking to Sven Ulven. I overheard Ulven tell him how Nichols pulled the wool over his eyes. That means only one thing – Carthage City is dead. The new town will be down in the valley. I'll be packing up and moving down there as soon as possible."

"Yes, I suppose we'll all be moving down there in the near future."

"I don't think we'll *all* be moving. I got the impression from listening to Hay and Ulven that Hay isn't quite ready to quit Carthage City. He's been burned pretty bad, Mordecai, and I don't think he's going to take it lying down. He's a desperate man, and he's liable to do anything to get even."

"What can he do, George?" contradicted Mordecai. "We've broken him. He's wasted his company's money. The men who've been working for him certainly won't follow him again, not after they hear what Russ did to him and especially not after the way he backed down yesterday. And his superiors are sure to remove him as soon as they learn about his fiasco here in Carthage City. No, George, I don't think we have to worry about Mr. Beecher Hay any longer."

True to his word, Hay wasn't finished. He burst into his office at the mill and passed through it to the storeroom in back. He reached into a vest pocket and removed a key as he stepped up to a tall, wooden cabinet. He unlocked the door, opened it, and revealed two cases of dynamite. He set himself to work binding four sticks of the explosive together and fitting them with fuses. Then he repeated the process three times. The task completed, Hay closed the door and locked it. He started for the office but was stopped.

"I'm sorry, my boy," said Hay. "I forgot you were here."

Jack Maler shook his head slowly and waved as if refusing the apology. The bandaged wound in his throat limited him talking. He pointed at the dynamite in Hay's hands.

"Oh, this. Those prospectors have tricked me, and now I'm going to ride down to the lumber mill and blow up the dam and drown them, just like the Lord did to Pharaoh's soldiers in the Bible."

Maler shook his head and forced a whisper. "Let . . . me . . . do . . . it."

"Why certainly, my boy." Hay smiled. "I'd be glad to let you have the honors." He handed the charges to Maler. "I'll get you a sack to carry them in."

Maler followed Hay into the office. Hay took an ore sack from a pile in the corner and held it open for Maler, who placed the four bundles of dynamite into it. Maler quickly returned to the storeroom for his gun, coat, and hat. He rejoined Hay.

"I wish it was night," said Hay. "You would be less likely to be seen if it was, but since it isn't, I want you to take the ore road around the slope and then the canyon road below the town. Is that clear, Jack?"

Maler nodded, then left.

Bemis wasn't the only person awakened by the conversation between Hay and Ulven. Louisiana Sal also had her slumber disturbed. She decided that since she was awake and no longer sleepy she might as well get up and do her exercises. Once they were out of the way, she went to the window and opened it. As she breathed in the cool mountain air, she saw someone leave the stamp mill. He was carrying a sack, and he climbed onto Hay's horse. There was something familiar about the man, but she couldn't quite figure out what it was. He turned the horse, and in so doing, his coat came open, revealing the grip of a gun. There was no mistaking it. The weapon was the silver-plated Smith & Wesson American .44 with the ivory handle that belonged to Jack Maler.

Sal gasped and rubbed her eyes, thinking that she had made a mistake. She stared harder at the man as he rode up the ore road. She still wasn't absolutely positive that it was Maler.

"If it isn't Maler," she asked herself aloud, "then who is it?"

Sal grabbed a dress and climbed into it. Attired, she stepped from her apartment and rushed down to the Bonanza Room. She saw Mordecai at the bar drinking coffee and talking to Bemis. She walked over to them.

"Well, you're up early, Miss Macomb," observed Mordecai. "It must be that kind of morning. First Hay, then George, and now you. Must be something in the air."

"You're right about that," said Sal. "There is something in the air, and I'm not sure what it is."

"Autumn is just around the corner," said Mordecai. "The changing seasons do have an effect on people, you know."

"That isn't it," said Sal. "Mordecai, didn't

you say you killed Maler the night your place burned down?"

The little man puffed up his chest. "I certainly did. I shot him right through the neck."

"Are you sure you killed him?"

"Of course, I'm sure."

"Well, I'll tell you, I think I just saw Maler leave Hay's stamp mill carrying a sack."

"It couldn't have been Maler," argued Mordecai. "I killed him, and his body was burned up in the fire."

"Are you sure?" queried Sal. "I mean, did you find any bones in the ashes? If his body was burned in the fire, there would have been some bones or some trace of him left in the ashes. Isn't that right, George?"

"I should think so," said Bemis. "Did you find anything like that, Mordecai?"

"No," admitted the journalist. "I didn't look through the ashes."

Sal looked at Bemis first, then Mordecai. "I'm beginning to think that it was Maler I just saw."

"Maybe we'd better go talk to Hay?" suggested Bemis.

"I think you've got something there, George," said Mordecai. "You'd better bring your rifle, and we'll get my gun on the way."

A few minutes later Bemis and Mordecai

were standing in Hay's office. The mining executive sat placidly at his desk.

"Hay, I came here once to kill you," said Mordecai, "but I didn't because Russ Nichols stopped me. Well, Russ isn't here now."

"Easy, Mordecai," warned Bemis. "There's no sense in getting excited just yet. Let's give Mr. Hay a chance to explain."

"Explain what?" asked Hay.

"Sal Macomb just told us she saw Jack Maler leave this office a few minutes ago."

"That's ridiculous," chortled Hay. "Maler is dead. You told me yourself, Mr. Courtney, that you killed him."

"That's what I thought, but now I'm not so sure."

Mordecai saw the pile of sacks in the corner, and he remembered Sal saying that the man she had seen was carrying one.

"George, look over there," said Mordecai as he pointed to the bags.

"Hm. Maybe we should have a look around."

"Hold on there," protested Hay. "You have no right . . ."

Bemis aimed his Winchester at Hay's face. "This gives us the right, Mr. Hay. Now I think we'll have a look around here. What's through that door?"

"That's just a closet," lied Hay.

Mordecai went around the desk and opened the door.

"Closet, you say?" chided Bemis. "What's in there, Mordecai?"

"A bed, a basin, and" — he returned to the office — "and these." He held up some bandages with dried blood crusted on a few of them. "Scratch yourself, Hay?"

"Then it was Maler," said Bemis. "Where was he going, Mr. Hay?"

"I tell you, Maler wasn't here."

"That's a lie," said Mordecai, "and you know it. Now tell us where he was going."

Hay laughed. "So you thought you could beat me, didn't you, inkslinger? Well, you haven't. I might as well tell you since Jack is well on his way and you can't stop him now."

"Out with it, Hay!" commanded Mordecai.

"Jack is on his way to blow up the dam at the sawmill."

"Blow up the dam?"

"That's right. All that water should make a lovely flood for your friends in the valley."

Hay broke into the laughter of a lunatic. Bemis and Mordecai exchanged confused stares. Hay's cackling made them realize that there was no time to waste. Without further words, they ran from the office. They made straight for Eldon's livery at the other end of

276

town. Fortunately, it was a downhill run.

Sven Ulven stepped out on the balcony of the Golden Palace Hotel. He saw Bemis and Mordecai running past.

"What's the hurry?" called Ulven.

"Maler is going to blow up the sawmill dam," answered Bemis.

"He can't do that," shouted Ulven.

"We know," shouted Mordecai, gasping for air. "All the men below will be drowned."

"I know," said Ulven, "but . . ."

He didn't finish the sentence because his listeners were out of earshot. Instead, Ulven rushed back into the hotel and downstairs. He met Louisiana Sal at the landing.

"Miss Macomb," panted Ulven, "there's serious trouble afoot. Jack Maler is alive."

"I know," said Sal.

"And he's going to blow up the sawmill dam," continued Ulven.

"That's terrible," said Sal with a hand to her mouth. "All those poor men down in the valley will be drowned."

"That isn't all, Miss Macomb. That dam is at the beginning of a large fault."

"A what?"

"A fault," explained Ulven. "A crack in the earth. If that dam is blown up, it might start a landslide on the slope that could destroy Carthage City."

"Oh, my God!"

"We've got to warn everyone."

"I'll get my girls to help."

Sal hurried up the stairs as Ulven ran outside. Sal bumped into Mallory in the hall.

"John, Maler is going to blow up the dam."

"I heard," said Mallory. "You go on. I'm going to try to catch Maler."

Eldon and his son had two horses saddled for Bemis and Mordecai within minutes after they entered the stable. They mounted up and kicked the steeds into motion. There was no time for caution on the steep canyon road as they urged the animals to full speed. Bemis was the better rider, so he moved ahead of Mordecai as soon as they were out of town. When the valley and the dam came into view, Bemis was a full hundred feet in the lead. They hadn't even made it a quarter of the way to the sawmill when Bemis's mount stepped into a chuckhole and fell, throwing the saloonkeeper to the ground. He rolled as best as he could but couldn't prevent his left arm from breaking above the wrist. The mare he was riding managed to get to her feet, but it was obvious that she had fractured a fetlock. Mordecai pulled up short of his comrade.

"Are you all right, George?"

"Never mind me. Get after Maler."

"Are you . . ."

"Damn it all, Mordecai, ride!"

The adrenaline in Mordecai's bloodstream was keeping his asthma in check, and his heart was maintaining the pace. He buried his heels into the gelding's ribs, and he was off again.

As he neared the halfway point, the echoes of three, maybe four, gunshots reached Mordecai's ears. Maler, he figured, must be having trouble with Julius Heintz or he was murdering the lumberman. Then Mordecai remembered that Heintz had a couple of men working for him. Maler could be killing all of them.

When Mordecai rounded the last bend in the road before the sawmill, he saw two men. One was Heintz, who was riding away from the dam toward the valley. The other was Maler. He was trying to mount Hay's horse to make his escape.

"Maler!" shouted Mordecai. The journalist drew his Remington as he pulled up the reins and halted the gelding.

Hearing his name called temporarily stopped Maler from getting into the saddle. He looked up at Mordecai. Hate contorted his features. He threw himself onto the horse's back. He drew his .44 and charged Mordecai.

The first shot came from Mordecai's .25, but it missed everything except the millpond to Maler's left. The gap between the two men was less than a hundred feet, but Mordecai, unlike Maler, didn't know that he was wasting bullets. He fired again, and again he missed.

At twenty-five feet, Maler cut loose a slug. It zinged by Mordecai's ear. Mordecai returned the fire, and Maler's hat flew off behind him. The gelding twisted and danced in the road, partially blocking Maler's path. Maler's next shot passed through Mordecai's pant leg, through the saddle fender, and into the horse's side, striking a rib but doing little damage to the animal. The sudden pain of the wound did scare the gelding into rearing. It came down directly in front of Maler's mount. The two beasts collided, and the gelding went down, spilling Mordecai. Maler's horse stumbled but stayed afoot.

Mordecai rolled over, the Remington still in his hand. He looked up to see Maler looming over him from the saddle, the .44 aimed at his chest. He heard the hammer fall and expected the barrel to spit fire and lead, but the only sound was a hollow click. Maler's gun was empty. Realizing his advantage, Mordecai pointed the .25 at Maler.

"You're finished, Maler!"

Maler kicked his horse's sides. It leaped ahead, but he toppled to the ground, a bullet through his left lung.

The blast from Bemis' Winchester startled Mordecai, but the sight of Maler writhing on the road less than ten feet from him frightened him even more. Maler was dying, but Mordecai didn't know that. The journalist wasn't sure what he should do — help Maler or shoot him?

The pounding of hoofs interrupted Mordecai's thoughts. Pinky John Mallory was riding toward him. The gambler stopped his horse just short of Maler. He put the stock of his rifle to his shoulder and aimed at the expiring gunman.

"Do you want me to end it, Maler?" asked Mallory in a steely cold voice.

Maler lifted his head to gaze through glassy eyes at Mallory. His lips moved momentarily, emitting gurgling blood. His head dropped back, and the bubbling sound ceased. Maler was dead.

Mallory lowered the Winchester. "No, I guess not."

Mordecai scrambled to his feet. "Mallory, the dam!"

There was nothing either of them could do. The first charge exploded and the remaining three followed in five-second intervals. Water and debris from the dam and mill were thrown high into the air, some of it splashing and crashing down around Mordecai and Mallory but doing them no harm.

The horses scattered, and both men threw themselves to the ground with the initial blast. After the last explosion, they stood up in time to see the millpond finish draining.

"My God!" swore Mordecai. "Those poor men below!"

"We can't help them," said Mallory, "but we can save those people in Carthage City."

"What are you talking about, Mallory?"

Before the gambler could answer, the land beneath them shook and rumbled. Again, they were down. Part of the road fell away into the creek bed. Trees cracked and fell. Boulders began tumbling down the canyon's steep sides, but none of them endangered Mordecai or Mallory.

The tremor was light at its source, but as the shock wave followed the geological fault of the canyon, it picked up strength. By the time it reached the slope above Carthage City, the quake had attained its most destructive force. Already weakened by the mining operations, the mountainside crumbled away easily.

Louisiana Sal and her girls had been successful at warning the townspeople about the impending disaster, and Ulven was able to get the men working in the mines out of them in time. By the time the landslide began, the people were all moving away from town. Only Beecher Hay had failed to receive the alarm.

By the reactions of the fleeing citizens, it seemed that the whole mountain was coming down on the community and would continue rolling the length of the canyon, destroying everything and everyone in its path. Tons of soil and rock slid from the slope toward Carthage City but not as much as imagined.

The stamp mill stood mute against the sliding earth but only for a moment. In seconds, the steam-powered crushers were themselves crushed, and the entire mining complex was leveled, including the office of Beecher Hay with him in it.

The slide, which had appeared to be so terribly awesome, suddenly died, damaging none of the other buildings. The more religious folks in town called it a miracle, but Ulven knew the real reason for the salvation of Carthage City. The stamp mill had been erected over the only solid spot in the area, and the earth beneath it had remained stable through the quake. Maybe that was divine intervention after all.

EPILOGUE

Julius Heintz had reached Russ Nichols and the other prospectors in time to save them from the wall of water rushing down the canyon, and every man staked a new claim in the foothills later that day.

Carthage City as a mountain mining town was dead. The men and women who had built it dismantled the community, moved it to the valley, and raised it up again.

In order to avoid a repeat of the events concerning Beecher Hay and the Southwest Arizona Mining Company, the miners formed their own corporation. They elected George Bemis to the position of chairman of the board, and Russ Nichols was made president. Sven Ulven stayed on as the new outfit's operations engineer.

Louisiana Sal Macomb married Russ Nichols, but her girls remained together long enough to perform on the Barbary Coast of San Francisco.

Pinky John Mallory stayed for a while, but he eventually grew restless and moved on to Arizona. He continued practicing his chosen profession.

And Mordecai Courtney? As much as he wanted to be wealthy, he was a miserable failure in business. Oh, the *Clarion* prospered well enough, but Mordecai mortgaged it too heavily, eventually losing it to the highest bidder.

As for Mordecai himself? He passed into history. Just like all the other inkslingers of the Old West, he left a rich and valuable archive in the numbers he printed. Through them, Mordecai Courtney became immortal.

Lakeside
EC
SenCit Ct
EC92
ΛC93
acs
B.F.J.
IL97
RH99
EEm
LCOI
RH05